Deceased
and Desist

Also by MISTY SIMON

Grounds for Remorse

Cremains of the Day

Deceased and Desist

Misty Simon

KENSINGTON PUBLISHING CORP.

www.kensingtonbooks.com

KENSINGTON BOOKS are published by

Kensington Publishing Corp.
119 West 40th Street
New York, NY 10018

All Kensington titles, imprints, and distributed lines are available at special quantity discounts for bulk purchases for sales promotions, premiums, fund-raising, educational, or institutional use. Special book excerpts or customized printings can also be created to fit specific needs. For details, write or phone the office of the Kensington sales manager: Kensington Publishing Corp., 119 West 40th Street, New York, NY 10018, attn: Sales Department; phone 1-800-221-2647.

ISBN-13: 978-1-4967-1225-7
ISBN-10: 1-4967-1225-0

First printing: December 2018

10 9 8 7 6 5 4 3 2 1

Printed in the United States of America

Electronic edition: December 2018

ISBN-13: 978-1-4967-1226-4
ISBN-10: 1-4967-1226-9

To all the musicians out there
who make my job sing with their voices,
their hearts, and their vibe.
I can't thank you enough!

And to Daniel and Noelle,
who never complain about the dishes
or pizza for the third time when I'm on a roll.

Chapter One

If I were being honest, and I usually was, at least with myself, I would say cleaning windows had always been one of my favorite things to do. Even when I was Mrs. Walden Phillips III and had someone come in to clean my big house, I would do the windows myself. There was something about using a squeegee to cut away the grime, the way you could see the difference between clean and dirty, and the sheer joy of a window that the sun bounced off of, that just made me happy.

During my marriage, there was little else that fell in that category, so sometimes I just had to take my happiness where I could find it.

Now that I was divorced and cleaning houses, cleaning windows still hadn't gotten old. I could do without vacuuming sometimes, or finding hidden socks in couches, cleaning up after people who couldn't even seem to get their glass three more inches into the actual sink, but window cleaning? I was your girl. Maybe I should have set myself up as Tallie Graver, Professional Window Cleaner, instead of Tallie Graver, Cleaning Woman. That decision was long gone now, though, and cleaning houses kept me in food and away from having to work full-time at my father's funeral parlor.

I was thankful that he let me come back to the family business after my fall from the upper class of our small town. Still, I had no desire to devote my life to dead people, as my father and my brother had done. And so I cleaned and found my pockets of happiness where I could.

It was especially hard to find those pockets of happiness when my boyfriend was not in the area, like this week, when he'd taken a flight to Hawaii for work without me. He'd asked me to come with him, but I didn't have the time. Being your own boss did come with some drawbacks, like having to work to make any money at all.

And so I was here, at the Crossing Bridge Inn, a beautiful, old stone inn on the outskirts of town, cleaning windows and smiling to myself.

The Central Pennsylvania day was gorgeous. A cool breeze came in from the north. November around these parts was never predictable, but this year was even weirder than normal. Last week there had been snow, yet this week it was seventy in the shade. Go figure. I'd take it, though. If it meant I could clean the windows outside the inn without a jacket and with the sun on my face, I was happy.

I did all the downstairs windows, and then went inside and up the sweeping staircase to the second story to do the back windows. A stained wood balcony ran the full length of the back and wrapped around the sides, making it very convenient to do the exteriors of the windows. Within an hour the old wavy glass was positively gleaming. Now on to the windows in the front. For those, I had to get a ladder.

Lugging my gear downstairs, I arrived in the kitchen to find Rhoda Monroe, the owner, cooking up a storm for the grand reopening this weekend. Pots bubbled on the old white stove, mixing bowls stood sentry on the tile counters, and pan after pan of baked goods took up the remaining countertops.

"Oh, Tallie! How are things? How's life? How are my windows?"

I laughed because every sentence could have been punctuated with an exclamation point instead of a question mark. Rhoda had a lot going for her, and the biggest plus was her enthusiasm for all things. She and her husband, Arthur, had gone through a rough time recently when the inn suffered water damage and had to be shut down to fix and renovate. They'd closed for six months while people stepped up to help with new floors and refurbishing the basement. Wallpaper was replaced, and Rhoda had taken the opportunity to put in a new kitchen. This was their first weekend open in half a year and the place looked fabulous. I loved that they were getting back into the swing of things.

"Everything is good, and the windows are gleaming. Not a speck of grime."

"Good, good! Can I mail you a check? My hands are covered with dough." She held them up so I could see she wasn't lying.

"Of course." Unlike some of my customers, I trusted that when Rhoda said the check was in the mail, it actually was. She'd been friends with my family for a number of years. When we had family events that required people to fly in from out of town, we always set them up at this inn. We'd used the one in town, too. Believe me, I had so many relatives they could fill the inn, the local hotel, and a chain hotel or two.

"Oh, thanks! I sure do appreciate that. Arthur is taking a nap before things start hopping, so I thought I'd get a jump on the baking for this weekend."

"It smells delicious." Almost better than my best friend Gina Laudermilch's baking, not that I would ever tell her that. And once Rhoda got into wedding season in a few months she often ordered from Gina to round out what she might not be able to produce herself. Gina had also catered functions here before the shutdown and had been contacted to start again. The sweeping lawn and old trees made the perfect backdrop for a wedding or really any special occasion.

This was my first time doing the windows here. I hoped I'd be here more often soon. For one, I now helped Gina as needed with her catering. For two, I really wanted the contract to clean the inn on a weekly basis. Until about two years ago catering was not something I did, neither was cleaning. I hired people for both. Now I was the hired help, and, surprisingly, I didn't mind one bit.

"Do you have a full house coming for your first weekend?" I asked, just to take a few more minutes to enjoy the smell of baking breads and muffins. With my small studio apartment above the funeral home my father owned, I didn't bake much, but I sure did love the smell of fresh-baked everything. I opened my windows whenever I could to get the scent from across the street at Gina's.

"Oh, I sure do. This weekend is a big one. Every

room is full. They're all due to arrive Friday afternoon, so I'm trying to get my baking out of the way."

"Of course."

"And then there'll be many other things to do. Just have to get all those cute ducks in a row."

"You'll do it. You've always been amazing at keeping things in order."

She smiled and kneaded whatever was in the bowl on the butcher block. "You're right there. Always was good at organizing and keeping things in line."

I'd wasted enough time and still had things to finish up. I waved to her and headed out the back door. As I passed my car, I put my jacket into the backseat, since I wasn't using it for the next part. I would be high up, which would make me sweat anyway, on a ladder and using a squeegee to clean grime off the front windows. A jacket would only make things worse. As a bonus, once I was done, I could head right back to the car and go without having to go back into the house.

Trekking to the huge garage, I waved to Paul, the gardener, and Annie, who led tours of the area for the inn. They were married and had lived in the carriage house on the back of the property for years. For as sleepy of a little town as we were, we were also pretty popular, especially because we were one of the major points where the Confederate troops had been turned around. Even our library was housed in a building that had been a hospital for the battles raging through the area over one hundred fifty years ago.

Using every muscle I had at my disposal, I pulled the big barn door toward me. The sucker was heavy. I had talked with Arthur about getting sliding doors, but he was all about authenticity. He even had times of the year that only candles burned in the rooms, no electricity. Not in November, of course, or people would have to wear heavy coats indoors instead of enjoying modern gas heat. But in the summer, when the sun didn't set until almost nine, he burned candles and had people here dressed in period costume who led ghost tours. I'd done one with Max several months ago, before the water damage, and it had been a blast.

I missed that man of mine and hoped I'd see him again soon. I didn't understand all the particulars of his business trip, and apparently he couldn't tell me all the juicy details. So, I talked with him on the phone as often as possible and we video chatted when he was able and I was free. For right now it was enough.

I had told him he should think about moving up my way from DC without actually inviting him to live with me. After that, the conversation had been tabled. I was feeling the loss, though, with this separation of well over a month. It was taking more of a toll on me than I had realized. We could function without being in each other's pockets every moment of the day, I knew that. But I missed him when he was so far away.

I waded through stacks of tables and chairs, bins stuffed with linens, and three mowers to get the ladder. The garage was actually a barn and stuffed to the rafters with all the things it took to run a successful inn. Rhoda and Arthur must have been extremely pleased to be able to put everything back to its proper use.

Hauling the ladder around the front of the house, I set it up at the first window. The ladder was metal and had a shelf three-quarters of the way up where I could rest my bucket. I scaled the rungs with the bucket in hand, hoping fervently that I wouldn't fall. To be fair, I probably wouldn't, but there could be a first time for everything. I just didn't want it to be today, or any day really, but certainly not today.

My best friend Gina and I had plans to stuff our faces with pizza and watch awesomely romantic movies. First up: *The Princess Bride.*

But not until I was done with these windows.

I arrived at the first of the fourteen windows on this level, gripped the edge of the top step and the squeegee tight and went to work removing the grime that had accumulated over the last several months. I spritzed and squeegeed, then spritzed and squeegeed again. The way the grime came off, leaving half the window clean and the other half hazy, was satisfying to say the least.

Slowly but surely I was able to see the room itself. Rhoda had made other upgrades during the renovation, putting new quilts on the beds and placing a bench at the footboard. The quilts were handmade from Amish country, per my mother, and the furnishings bought from an estate sale up the road.

No matter where Rhoda had gotten what, she'd made each space so individual it would be like sleeping in your own bedroom but with someone to clean up after you and make your breakfast. Not a bad deal, plus Rhoda's cooking was worth every penny.

I heard a car pull into the lot, followed by another. Probably the last of the repair people to make sure the inn was ready to go in four days. It would be so nice to have the old girl up and running.

Hopefully Rhoda was done kneading whatever had

been in that bowl so she could greet them. If not, I was sure Annie would be right in.

This cleaning, and jobs like this, were gravy on my plate of delicious french fries. Not too much work, mainly general areas with dusting and vacuuming and then the bedrooms. The personal quarters Rhoda and Arthur had set up she cleaned on her own. I called a win-win when she'd decided to give me a shot at the contract when they reopened.

Sparkly windows always put major points in my favor, if I could just get them all done.

After I finished with the first window I moved to the next and the next, humming to myself and smiling. I probably looked ridiculous fifteen feet up, swiping and smiling. But who cared? Not me. Life was good and was only getting better.

On the fourteenth window, I placed the ladder right under it, but the thing rocked. No way was I going to go up fifteen feet on a rocky ladder. *Crap.*

Inspecting the ground, I found a few soft spots with the toe of my sneaker and worked the ladder around until I found a more solid place. Now that I'd finally found a spot where I didn't think I was going to fall on my face when I climbed the thing, I inched it around a few times until it stopped teetering. It would do. Once I had it firmly in place, I scaled that bad boy, knowing it was only about thirty minutes until I could call it a day and order my enormous pizza.

This window got the brunt of the grime from the road. The stone inn was turned at a forty-degree angle to the road, which gave it ambience and a clear path to the small bridge made from stone that had crossed the creek for centuries. The bridge was original, built in the time of the first colonists, and, except for the covered bridge a mile away, it was one of the things locals often saw and didn't notice but tourists loved.

The creek it spanned gurgled along swiftly for this time of year, no more than a foot deep in most places, but when the rains came it rose two to three times that depth. People gleefully kayaked on it in the summer.

I thought about trying that out every year but ended up never wanting to get into the water. Max kept talking about kayaking because it was something he loved to do. I kept putting him off without an explanation. That might not last forever. At some point I was either going to have to own up to not wanting to go because I was scared of the water, or just give in and at least try it. Knowing me it would be the latter. But there was nothing wrong with some new experiences.

Being in love, truly in love, was a first for me this time around, and I hadn't died from the experience yet.

I glanced down into the water, watched a cluster of leaves float by and heard some kind of animal scurry through the undergrowth on the banks, then got to work. It might be pleasant weather now, but that could change in a flash. It was still November, even if I was out here in a shirt with no jacket.

Taking my first swipe, I cleaned away the grime. To my frustration, it didn't come all the way off. I went for it again, and made some headway, but it still wasn't clean.

I did another swipe and then went over that again, and that small spot was finally clean. The act mimicked me shaving my legs after a long winter and made me giggle. I immediately silenced myself when I saw someone on the other side of the glass.

I thought there weren't any guests at the inn. According to Rhoda, everyone was arriving later on Friday and it was only Monday. But there was a guy sound asleep on the bed, his head turned toward me.

I caught the tail end of the door closing out of the corner of my eye. Someone I couldn't see left the room and left the guy to his nap. Maybe Rhoda, making sure her guest was comfortable. I knew it wasn't Arthur on the bed since their rooms were downstairs behind the kitchen. Also, this man had dark hair while Arthur had a fabulous, brilliant-silver comb-over.

After my next swipe, I realized something looked wrong about this guy.

And then I looked harder and squeegeed some more, working furiously to get the grime to go away to get a clearer picture. The guy wasn't sleeping. His eyes were wide open, and he hadn't blinked the entire time I'd been working on the window. His head was at an impossible angle, turned so I could see his face and also his back. Totally unnatural. As if I needed more proof, his eyes were blank.

With this being my life, of course he wasn't just taking an impromptu nap. He was dead. And whoever had just walked out had probably killed him.

I stifled a shriek, not wanting to rock the ladder. A dead body. Again. I should get down the ladder, snag Rhoda, or at least tell her what had happened if she didn't want to see a dead body. Not that I wanted to see one either, but between the three murders that I'd solved over the last year, and the fact that I worked at a funeral home part-time, I kind of couldn't avoid them.

I'd talk to Suzy at the police station while they came to get him and I wouldn't touch a thing, I promised myself. After the last two times, I had learned my lesson.

But then I realized that doing it that way would take way too much time. Instead, I scrambled halfway down the ladder, then looped my arm through the rungs. Grabbing my phone out of my back pocket, I steadied myself. If I started the phone call now, I could back the rest of the way down while talking. I didn't have much choice. Once I got on the ground I could talk better, but for right now I at least had to report this. Awkwardly hitting the speed dial with my pinkie, I then held the phone to my ear, standing on tiptoe to keep an eye on the dead guy in the Mummer Suite.

And so I wasn't prepared, nor was I able to do anything about it, when the ladder teeter-tottered. It went to the right and I went to the left. To my horror, I flew through the air with nothing to save me. Almost like my swan dive from grace with the upper crust of this town. It was a split-second thought and one that winged out of my head as the ground came up way too fast to greet my face and anything else I might hit.

Hitting the grass with a yell, my first thought was what had I broken? Please let it be nothing. As I lay prone in the crunchy grass, I assessed the damage without moving too much. Thank heavens the ground was spongy from the snowmelt last week. I had landed on a soft spot.

I had survived, but the man upstairs hadn't. I needed to call this in before any more time passed.

I'd get yelled at by Police Chief Burton, of course,

but that was to be expected. First, I needed to catch my breath and take it slow.

My hip felt like it was on fire, though, and my shoulder and wrist hurt like someone had kicked me. I tried testing out all my working parts to see if they were still working and found that for the most part I was good to go. I stayed still for a moment, closing my eyes just to get my bearing.

Unfortunately, I must have passed out at some point because there was no slow coming around, no gradual awakening until I was ready to sit up. Someone splashed water in my face. My first foggy thought was that maybe it was raining. My second thought was that I hoped they hadn't used the dirty water from my bucket.

I came up sputtering and spitting, just in case.

Chapter Two

Rhoda stood over me with a frown marring her usually smiling face. I tried to frown, too, but it hurt too much so I stopped.

"You just lay still there, missy. I called the ambulance. We can't have you traipsing around if you're hurt. I'm so sorry for whatever happened. I heard a crash and I came to find you on the ground. Are you okay?"

Truthfully, I was nauseous and afraid to ask if the brackish taste in the back of my throat was because she really had used the dirty water in the bucket.

With a hand on my back, she helped me sit up. Once I was in an upright position I felt like my brain fell back into place. My synapses all started firing at once.

"Oh, my God, Rhoda! We're going to need two ambulances, and we need to run upstairs right now!" I had apparently taken up her overuse of exclamation points in my injured state.

"What? Why?"

"I was cleaning the front windows."

"Oh, I was wondering." She glanced up. "Great job, honey! So shiny! I thought you had gone home and had no idea where the noise came from until I ran outside from the kitchen."

"Yeah, I just stopped in the kitchen on my way out to the garage." I rubbed the back of my head where I was pretty sure a lump was forming. "When I was cleaning, though, I saw a guy in the front bedroom on the east side of the building and it looked like he was dead."

Her hands flew to her mouth. "But there's not supposed to be anyone here! Why would someone not only be here, but be dead, too?"

I tried to shrug my shoulders and that hurt as well. "I have no idea, but we'd better go check things out and call the police."

"Oh, my land's sakes. This is not good, not good at all. I should go wake up Arthur."

I took my cue that she was not particularly interested in seeing a dead body. I didn't blame her.

"Don't touch anything but your husband," I warned her. "And while you do that, I'm going to call the police again."

She ran off before I could finish my sentence, which was fine by me. One less person around trying to tell their story while I told mine would make this easier. Or at least that's the lie I told myself. Experience had taught me that nothing about finding a dead body was easy. Especially when I had to go up against Police Chief Burton.

After I picked up my phone from the ground, I realized the initial call had never gone through. It was probably better that way, since I had passed out.

If I'd called the emergency number and then not said a word, or only screamed on my way down to the ground, the police would be swarming right now. All four of them.

Suzy at the station picked up the call on the third ring. "Tallie, please tell me this is a traffic accident or something."

Nerves rang through Suzy's voice and her normally loud volume was almost a whisper. I probably could have figured out why, but with my addled brain and the fact that I hurt from head to toe, I was in no mood to get crap for finding another body. There was no way around it, though. "Someone is dead at the Crossing Bridge Inn."

"And you just happened to find them?" She blew out a breath. "Why do I even ask? Of course you did." She put a hand over the phone, but I still heard her yell out to someone in the office to get the heck over to the inn pronto and call the coroner.

Well, at least the police would be on their way. Now if I could just get Suzy off the phone. "Okay, message delivered. I'm going to go upstairs just to keep a watch on the room until you guys arrive."

"No," she yelled. After a moment, her voice dropped back down to almost a whisper, as if she'd realized she needed to keep quiet. But why? "Seriously, Tallie, if you never listen to me again, please at least listen to me now. You're going to stay right where you are. Do not move a muscle. The chief won't want contamination of the scene, and your part of this is now officially over."

I could have sputtered. Instead, I decided to stay silent. This would actually be better. I'd get checked by the paramedics Rhoda had called and then go have my movie night. I was sure I was fine. And the police could handle this, I told myself sternly. I'd simply call Gina and tell her to hold the movie for a few more minutes.

That was wishful thinking, though.

The paramedics screamed up the driveway in their shiny new ride that they'd fund-raised for with calendars of hot men in uniform. Just to keep it interesting they had also asked the local senior living home if they had some women interested in posing with them. The calendar was a wonder of awesomeness and raised enough money that the senior center also got a new van of its own. I bought three of those calendars.

Roy, Mr. July, came trotting up with his gear, smiling at me. "Tallie Graver. I jumped right in the truck when I heard it was you."

I rolled my eyes. This guy had teased me mercilessly throughout all of our school years, from preschool to senior year.

"What did you do?" he asked as he used a penlight on my eyes, telling me to track the light.

"Fell off a ladder."

"All the way from the second story?" He felt the back of my head, rotated my shoulder and then tested my wrists.

"No, I was halfway down."

"You have to be more careful. You don't have a concussion, so that's good. And everything seems to be working fine, but you should still go to the hospital. You can take a ride in our brand-new ambulance."

Not if I could help it. I immediately began coming

up with excuses. I settled on the easiest one. "I think I'm going to be okay. I wasn't that high up."

"When you do it, you do it right." Roy stared up to the second-floor windows and whistled.

I didn't need kudos. I needed a clear bill of health so I could get out of here. "Thanks. I won't need a trip to the hospital, but your ambulance should be good for the dead body upstairs."

His jaw dropped, the smile completely gone. "You have to be kidding. Another one? What is that, six now?"

"Four, counting this one, doofus." I crossed my arms over my chest, being careful of my wrist.

After rubbing his chin, he smirked. "Ah, just four."

"I swear I was on the other side of the glass from this one this time."

"Chief's not going to be happy." Roy checked my pulse with cold hands.

Like I didn't already know that. I had endured it before, I could certainly endure it again. "I'm pretty sure I see him coming now. He can be unhappy with me in person after he checks out the dead guy upstairs." Jumping up from the bumper of the ambulance, I said a hurried goodbye as Roy tried to continue examining me. I walked away just as a man emerged from a police cruiser.

Thankfully it was my cousin, Matt, instead of Burton. I was still feeling a little wobbly and preferred not to have a confrontation at this point, no matter what I had said to Suzy.

"Tallie, should I even ask?" Sticking his hands into his uniform pants' pockets, Matt rocked back on his shiny black shoes.

"You just did." Unlike with Burton, cheeky was well received here. Matt shook his head at me and chuckled without a trace of anger in his expression.

Then he got down to business. Moving to my left, he took in the scene. The ladder on its side, me listing to the right, the dirty bucket overturned. God, she had used the dirty water. I was in serious need of a shower. I was never so happy that I used natural products for windows and had left out the ammonia or I would be burning from head to toe right now on top of the soreness setting in.

After a handful of seconds, he looked at me again. "You okay?"

It was nice of him to ask. Burton would have been a severe thundercloud with undertones of a tornado. I shrugged. It didn't hurt as much this time, just a twinge. "I was in the middle of having Roy, the clown, check when you pulled up. What do you want to know first?" I sat on a beautiful stone bench Rhoda had put at the front of the property, surrounding it with shrubs that bloomed in the spring and fall. Thank goodness I hadn't fallen in these. I would have had scratches to match the aching. It was bad enough that my hip was still burning.

"Just point out which room, get checked out with Roy, and go home. I promise I'll handle the rest."

I opened my mouth to ask if he wanted the time or the details of how I found the guy, but another police cruiser pulled up and Matt's whole demeanor changed in a flash. Instead of smiling and joking with me, Matt stood at attention, his eyes serious, and waited with his notebook in hand. I would have expected this from Burton, but not Matt.

What on earth had just happened?

"Just the bare facts and then I'll take it from here," he said in a loud voice.

I raised an eyebrow and prepared for battle. "But, normally—"

"There is no normally right now," he grated out in a much lower voice. "Just the facts and then be on your way. If I need further information I'll call you down to the station for a statement."

Okay, then. I would not be participating. I would not help. I would only give the bare minimum. Maybe I should just point and grunt instead of using real words. Because, obviously, I was not needed here at all. In any fashion. *Thanks for finding the dead body, Tallie, but now you can go on your merry little way.*

Fine by me. Whatever they wanted. I knew when I was being dismissed. I had a movie to watch whose main character said things such as "As you wish" and made my heart melt.

In the end, I did not resort to grunting, but it was close. "Up there. On the bed."

"Thank you." He sounded so relieved I didn't jump in with my own theories and thoughts, that I let it slide. At least for now.

There would be time to take him to task later when my head stopped pounding.

"Now, go let Roy do the rest of the checkup." Matt said. "You really should go to the hospital, but I'd settle for letting Roy finish his job."

I turned back to Roy, who smiled, waving a blood

pressure cuff and a stethoscope in his big hands. I really wanted him to give me a pain reliever and go away, but there was little hope of that actually happening. So, I sat for the rest of the exam on pins and needles, wondering if Matt would tell me anything when he came back downstairs. What was he finding right now?

Because of the shock and then the ladder fall, I'd had little time to register more than the guy lying with his eyes open and the severe angle of his neck. Who was it? Everything was so jumbled in my head that I felt like I was missing something.

"Ow!" I jerked my arm back from Roy's grip.

"Your wrist is at least sprained. It doesn't look broken, or feel broken, but there's something not right in there."

That seemed to be the thought of the day. Something not right.

"Can't you just give me one of those wrap things and let me go on my way?" Whining could get you many places if done right.

"I really think you need an X-ray, Tallie. I wouldn't mess with this if I was you. The bump on the back of your head should be looked at, too."

Being that I no longer had insurance through Waldo, my ex-husband, my father had given me employee insurance, even though I only worked part-time. But I had opted for the lowest possible premium, which meant I had the highest possible co-insurance and deductible.

I did not want to pay three hundred dollars at the emergency room to find out my head would be better with some aspirin and my wrist needed one of those

ACE Bandages from the local pharmacy. I could claim this as a worker's compensation case, but then my premium would go sky-high and I'd still pretty much be paying everything myself.

To top it all off, I certainly didn't want to pay for an ambulance ride. I hadn't subscribed to the ambulance fund this year and in these parts that meant I'd have to pay anything my insurance didn't cover.

"I'll go to urgent care."

He frowned, and I frowned back.

"I promise to go. I'll even have Gina drive me so I don't use my wrist too much. Okay?"

He still didn't look happy, but that wasn't my problem.

I jumped down off the edge of the ambulance bumper for the second time and let him put a bandage on me. No sling, thanks. Those made me feel too restrained.

I was done here and disappointed that Matt hadn't even come out to thank me for calling this in, or at least shared who the dead man was.

I walked to my car to get my jacket and a few other things, calling Gina on the way.

"I guess this is going to be more than a few minutes," she said.

"Well, hopefully urgent care isn't too busy, and then I promise we'll get to the movie."

"It's not the movie I'm worried about. It's you. Are you okay? Are you sure you shouldn't go to the hospital?"

"I'm fine, really. It's just urgent care and then we can get to our evening. I feel fine, but I have to keep my promise to Roy."

"And what about the police? Aren't they pissed that you found another body?"

"It's not as if I go looking for them." My hackles were up, I admit, but I was tired and sore and cranky. I crunched across the dry grass, then stepped on the resurfaced driveway.

"Don't get all defensive. I'm not saying you do, but this is becoming a habit. One you might want to break. You are at least staying out of it this time, right?"

"Of course," I said with far more conviction than I felt. If it was someone I knew, and it looked like the police weren't paying attention, then I made no promises about not at least looking around a little. But I was definitely going to leave this to Burton and his people to figure out. For now.

I'd reached my car, wedged between a maroon sedan and one of those tiny cars that looked like only clowns would come out of them. Opening my door just a smidgen, I reached in for my jacket and my purse. "Anyway, can you come pick me up? It appears I'm not needed here at the moment. If Rhoda wants me to come back for that last strip of window, I can do that later."

"Ten minutes."

"I'll be ready."

I locked my old Lexus, one of the few things I'd kept after the divorce, and headed back to the front of the house. This way Gina would only have to stop long enough for me to hop in the car, and then we could be on our way.

As I rounded the corner, Matt was waiting for me with another man who really did have thunderclouds rolling across his face that turned into threatening tornado bursts when he laid eyes on me.

"I swear I didn't touch anything," I said quickly, tucking my arms around my waist. "I didn't even go in the house after I found the dead body."

"Tallie, this is Detective Hammond."

"Okay," I said, not sure if I should try to shake the guy's hand. And also not sure why I was being introduced. Those storm clouds were very hateful, though.

"I know who she is, and I want her to stay out of this." His light blond hair fairly bristled off his head and his eyes were the iciest blue I'd ever had the misfortune to see.

"I have no intention of being in *this*," I snapped. "I didn't even go in the room. I saw him through the window." Irritated was an understatement. I was used to Burton being resigned, or even pissed, but not this anger towering over me. I took a step back just so he wasn't throwing a shadow on me. Who was he, anyway? A detective? But where did he fit into our department?

"I will have you in jail so fast your head will spin, Ms. Graver, if you even think about looking into anything having to do with this natural death." He flipped the edge of his jacket back and rested his hand on what I assumed was a gun holster. "It's a heart attack, not a murder, and you will stay far away from me and the department, or you'll pay. Dearly. Do we understand each other?"

No, we did not understand each other. How did he know it was a heart attack just from looking at the guy? Had he even looked at the guy? I clearly remembered his neck being wrong. Even though I didn't

often help with the bodies that came in to Graver
Funeral Home, I at least knew that if I could see your
back, I shouldn't also be able to see your face. "What
about the position of the body?"

"And that's the kind of question that will get you
tossed into jail." Hammond's jaw clenched and his
ears went back.

Matt stood behind this menace, making cutting
motions at his throat like he wanted me to stop. I was
fine with not being involved, but I knew what I had
seen and it most certainly wasn't a heart attack.

At least I didn't think so. Things were fuzzy, and I
still felt like I was missing something.

I despised how I was being treated, though, as if I
really did bring this on myself. So, I ignored Matt's
gesture and went with my gut. "His neck has been
broken. That doesn't happen with a heart attack.
And what was he doing in the room? He didn't just
walk in and then decide to have a heart attack at an
inn that isn't even open yet. I think something fishy is
going on."

He narrowed his eyes, closing the gap between us
to throw that shadow over me again. "Nothing is
going on here except the unfortunate death of a man.
I have seen him and the coroner will agree. And you
will heed my warning if you have any sense at all. This
was a heart attack, Ms. Graver. You will respect my
authority, or you'll find yourself dressed in orange
and running a metal cup over bars while you wish you
had some of that fancy coffee you seem to consume
by the gallons."

How the heck did he know about my coffee habit
when I only knew his name? And that was only because

we'd just been introduced. The words burned on my tongue to ask Matt who in the world this was. I knew the four police officers in town, and I'd never seen this one. Was he new? Where was Burton?

That last question I asked.

"Burton is temporarily out of commission due to an injury. I'm the interim chief and even if you don't respect him, you will respect me and my word. Now get out of here. Be warned that if I find you snooping in anything I will lay down the law. We are a clean and inviting town and your habits of finding dead people and making it into a fiasco will not happen on my watch. Or any watch again, if I have anything to say about it."

Chapter Three

"Why are you threatening me? You don't even know me, and I certainly don't know you." Not the most intelligent thing to say, but I really couldn't pinpoint anything else with the sheer amount of questions whirling in my head.

"This was not a murder. Go home." Hammond said it slowly as if I were having trouble comprehending basic words.

"I heard you. But how is that possible? I saw the guy. I saw him lying there with his eyes wide open and his neck broken. I did not imagine that." I hated repeating myself, but this guy, whoever he was, was not getting the picture.

The surly officer just shook his head as if I was living in a delusional world. "I am not going to agree with you in this instance. It was straight when I saw him. The man was here doing his job and had a heart attack. He was older and has a history of heart disease. Now move along."

What was going on?

"Who is it?" I knew I shouldn't have asked even before the words cleared my teeth, but I couldn't help myself.

"And that's precisely the kind of thing you do not need to know. Get in your car, Ms. Graver, and get out of here. I will be handling this. I certainly don't need some amateur trying to make it more than it is." His hands went to his hips like he was talking to a toddler. I did not need to be talked down to, but I hesitated, trying to recall any details other than the open eyes.

"I'm done talking about this. I've responded to your last question. I have nothing more to say. Unless you were the one who killed him since you're so sure that it was murder?" He peered closely at me. I so wanted to take another step back.

I made myself stand still, ignoring the urge.

"Explain that." He stared me down, and I had no idea what to say except to repeat myself, again, which I was not going to do.

But I knew what I had seen!

"That's ridiculous. I was cleaning the windows and then fell off the ladder. Rhoda found me on the ground."

"And yet, according to Mrs. Monroe, she was under the distinct impression that you had left."

"I said goodbye only because I didn't intend to come back in after I cleaned the upstairs windows out front."

"So your time is unaccounted for." That was a statement, not a question, and I was starting to feel distinctly under attack. Matt stuck his hand over his eyes, shaking his head.

Time to retreat. "Fine, it was a heart attack. I'm sorry for the family's loss."

Gina pulled up in her snazzy little sedan just as I decided not to fight it anymore. I was getting nowhere except closer to a jail cell fast. However, I had been wracking my brain for who the guy was, and I was pretty sure I had a name. If nothing else I'd at least check to see if it truly was Eli St. James who was no longer among the living, breathing his stinky breath and making people's life hell as a code enforcement professional. He'd liked to take bribes and fail your inspection if you weren't willing to pay. I needed to know if he had any business being at the inn, and if not, what had he been doing here?

After asking again if I was really okay, Gina asked about the body when I got in the car. Of course she did. After telling her I didn't know what to think, she let it go. Or tried to at least. Every few seconds, she kept glancing at me. Just to see if I was going to pass out? I had no idea, but I had a lot of thinking to do and no time to do it before we went into urgent care.

Situated in a renovated house on the corner of Fox and Clover Streets, the office served many of the people in town for bumps and bruises. If you needed to be seen without the fuss of trying to make an appointment three months out or didn't have a life-threatening emergency, this was the place to be.

Fortunately, the place wasn't full so I was seen

right away. Must have been a slow day for bumps and bruises.

Teresa Malloy was quick and efficient, and she didn't mince words when I asked if a person could have a twisted neck after a heart attack.

"It could have happened, I suppose, if he fell when he had the heart attack." She touched the back of my head and I winced. "That's going to hurt. Just put some ice on it and you should be fine." She shone a light in my eyes. "New body at the family biz?"

"Uh, no. I saw a body at the inn before I fell off the ladder." Seated on the crinkly paper covering the exam table, I swung my legs back and forth in little arcs. Examining rooms made me uncomfortable.

"Tallie. You need to stop getting involved with these things. You need a hobby or something."

I wasn't going to argue with her, but I certainly wasn't going to get a hobby. I had enough to do without trying to learn to crochet, and I had no garden to put flowers in. Hopping off the table, I thanked her for the splint and for not giving me a sling. She did call in a prescription for some pain meds that I probably wouldn't take. Last time I took anything more powerful than over-the-counter pain meds I'd felt like I was in a waking coma. I could hear everything, smell everything, but I couldn't open my eyes or talk. Not worth it.

"Make sure you fill this and take it as necessary, Tallie. I'm going to call Bart at the pharmacy and make sure you do."

There went that plan. But it didn't mean I had to take it.

"And I can call your mom and make sure you take it."

Good God, that would be fatal for everyone involved.

"I promise to take it. Please don't call my mom." And why did I suddenly feel ten?

"Good. Now don't do a lot with that left hand. You need to rest it."

"What about my house cleanings?" That was my livelihood.

"Ask Letty to take some over and move others. She did an amazing job on my house the other day. I would recommend her to anyone. She was a great addition to your company."

She absolutely was and had allowed me to go to Washington, DC, to shack up with Max a handful of weekends over the last several months.

"I'll call her when I leave."

"Make sure you do. I'm going to talk to her tomorrow when she calls to schedule her next cleaning for me. I'm going to make a note to myself to ask."

Lordy. "I will. Now can I go? I have pizza and movies in my future. I'd like to get started."

"If it doesn't get better call me or come back to see me."

"Fine, fine. I will. I'm sure you'll call my mom to check and see how I'm doing."

"Of course I won't. That would be a violation of HIPAA."

I didn't even argue about that point since calling about the meds would be the same thing. I just wanted to get out of here and start researching the man on the bed.

Once I got back in the car with Gina, I told her I needed another half hour at home. I wanted a shower immediately. More, I wanted my computer. I had a feeling she would have a fit if I decided to investigate this death. So, it was better done on my own time.

After hustling through my shower, I went to the computer and looked up Eli St. James. Only a few things came up with his name and a bunch of stuff that of course had nothing to do with him. That's the way of the internet.

His office was located on Braden Street in a strip mall and still showed as open, so I took a chance and called. A woman answered.

"St. James gets it done right," she said.

"Hi, I was looking for Mr. St. James."

"Oh, he left for the day a little while ago, called to say he wasn't coming back to the office after his last job."

"And where was his last job?"

"Let me see here."

I heard keys clacking away as she hummed to herself in that way certain people have. It didn't bother me until I realized she was humming a Barry Manilow song. My aunt did that and clicked her false teeth to the beat.

"You still there?" she asked. As if I would have hung up while I was waiting for an answer to my question.

"Yep, I'm still here. Where did you say his last appointment was?"

"Well, that's the problem. It doesn't say he had any appointments today. His schedule is clear. Hmm."

Hmm, indeed. No appointments and now he was dead at the inn where he had no business being? And why had Hammond said he was there doing his job? Why hadn't Rhoda mentioned that the inspector was on the grounds or in one of the rooms where I would be cleaning the windows?

"What time did he call to say he wasn't coming back?" I asked.

There was a pause, one I didn't have a good feeling about. And my gut was right once again.

"Who did you say you were? Eli's a good man. He shouldn't be in any trouble. You people need to leave him alone. He's only doing his job."

"I wasn't—" But she cut me off.

"Don't call here again. I have your number now. I'll report you to the police if you don't leave that poor man alone." And she hung up on me.

I did not need the police calling me, as I had a feeling they'd be doing it anyway. I was going to get some kind of follow-up about my report of a body from Burton, after Hammond reported to him, or a lecture on keeping my investigational tendencies to myself.

Matt could at least call and see if I was okay after my fall. I hadn't heard from him yet, either, and wanted to talk about the interim chief's ridiculous claim of a natural occurrence.

Nothing else popped up on the internet. I still didn't believe it had been a heart attack, but maybe once the coroner's report came back it would provide proof that I wasn't wrong.

Time to call through the network and see if one of my relatives knew the guy and why someone would want him dead. And if there were no clear answers then I'd leave it alone. If they ruled it a heart attack, I didn't want to waste my time hunting around when there was nothing to find.

As I went through the tree of aunts and uncles, cousins and distant cousins, I was surprised no one knew him, other than to tell me to stay away from him. Since I didn't want my questions to get back to my parents, I'd hang up instead of trying to explain my interest during each call. My dad would have a fit and my mother would probably faint.

I was running out of time and had nothing new to show for it. Gina had texted me twice already, and the second time threatened to come over to get me if I didn't hurry up. Plus, she told me she'd already ordered the pizza, which would arrive in fifteen minutes.

I took a chance and called Suzy at the station.

"I hear you had a mishap today," she said in that whisper again. Normally she was robust and quick to say what she meant and how she meant it. So why did I feel as if we were telling secrets?

Nice. A mishap. "Which part? Falling off the ladder or seeing a dead guy?"

"Both. You might want to lie low for a little while. The guys were not happy about you being at yet another crime scene and meddling yet again. Detective Hammond was not amused when he came back to the station."

"I swear I didn't make it up." I crossed my heart with my pinky even though she couldn't see it.

"I'm sure there was a dead body but not a murder, Tallie. Did you get your head checked? Maybe something got jarred loose."

And that's what I got for trying to talk with Suzy.

Although she had taken my calls before, she wasn't always the most helpful of people.

"I did have my head checked out, and I know what I saw. I guess I'll just have to look into this myself."

"Now, Tallie, don't go starting any trouble."

"Bye, Suzy."

"Seriously, Tallie, Burton is out of commission for a few weeks after that takedown near the paint factory. He's not in the best of moods lately due to that and the budget cuts. If he finds out you're snooping around about something that doesn't even exist, he is going to flip his lid. Not to mention Hammond will have you on the rack before you can blink. It's his MO."

"Who is Hammond? I've never seen him before."

"Well, you will now over the next six weeks. He's here from Chambersburg filling in for Burton, and it promises to be an interesting month and a half, if nothing else. He takes no prisoners, from what I heard through the cop grapevine. Don't get on his list."

"So don't tell him." I pushed the off button on my phone though it was never as satisfying as slamming the receiver back on the cradle of an old-style phone.

Where else could I get info? Someone had to know Eli St. James. I knew him vaguely but that was about it. How could he live in this town and not be known by any of my relatives?

When I glanced at my phone I realized the pizza would be delivered in two minutes.

Grabbing my purse and my keys, I made sure Mr. Fleefers had food and water, then high-tailed it out of my third-floor apartment above the funeral parlor my father owned. I worked there part-time but continued to fend off his offers to make me a full-time employee. I admired what my father, and my brother, did for a living, but I had no intention of devoting my life to the dead. I preferred cleaning up after the living. Dirty socks and all.

After jogging down the stairs and avoiding my mother, who was for some reason singing in the kitchen of the funeral home even though we'd closed an hour ago and hadn't had any services today, I made it out onto the street. And there was Gina just about to jaywalk to me. A cop car zoomed by, keeping her from actually crossing the street, and she grimaced at me as I walked halfway down the block to use the crosswalk then back up her side of the street to meet her.

"Took you long enough and your hair isn't even dry. What were you doing up there? Having a chat with the boyfriend?"

I hadn't even called Max to tell him about today. He had meetings and was in a different time zone. At this point, tomorrow was soon enough. I had nothing to report and only my own guesses to go on.

"My mom was in the kitchen."

That was enough to have her groaning. I hadn't actually lied, so I left it at that. The pizza delivery guy showed up and we stood out on the street to take it from him instead of making him follow us up the stairs only to send him back down.

The pies smelled heavenly, and yes, there were two of them, even though there were only two of us. Gina preferred pineapple and ham, and I couldn't abide that. Usually we split a pizza but that was when she'd get something normal, like sausage, or even just the ham, or ground beef. But pineapple was not something I could handle. Making it half had gone seriously wrong the last time when the pineapple juice had slid onto my side.

I followed her up the stairs, closing my eyes for a second as I remembered how she had found one seriously delusional admirer dead at the bottom just a few months ago. We'd put it behind us, but seeing the dead guy today brought it all back. I'd seen many a heart attack, and I did not ever remember seeing a tilted neck like that. I could ask my dad, but that would only bring about issues and questions I wasn't ready to deal with.

Better to eat my pizza, mind my own business for the night, and go in with my super-silent, almost nonexistent skills, tomorrow. It would be soon enough. Hopefully.

Chapter Four

Westley just wasn't doing it for me this evening. I adored the way he thwarted Prince Humperdinck and his best-known line. I especially loved seeing Andre the Giant and Inigo Montoya, but I just couldn't get the dead guy out of my mind. Was it really Eli? Was I just putting a name to the face that I hadn't seen that well before the ladder had started tipping?

Gina was completely engrossed in the movie even though this was one that we'd probably seen one hundred fifty-seven times. But it gave me the opportunity to think on my own for at least the next forty-five minutes. And a comfortable place to do it since Gina had couches, which I would have loved to have, but they wouldn't fit in my tiny apartment across the street. Chewing on the pizza, I also chewed on my thoughts.

I didn't like where they were going. Why was Hammond so dead set on a heart attack? Pun intended. How could he diagnose a heart attack at a glance? Sure there were signs, but he couldn't know for certain. He just couldn't!

I disliked him intensely, to say the least. And it was

concerning that everyone seemed to be afraid of him. Why?

I wished I'd been able to go into the room before heading out, but after being told off by Hammond and with Roy waiting for me to get a ride, I hadn't had a chance. Maybe I could squeeze in a visit tomorrow under the guise of making sure Rhoda and Arthur were okay. That was a phenomenal idea! And I would have to pick up my car. An even better excuse!

"You're not even watching," Gina said, breaking into my thoughts. "You always laugh at the 'mawwage' part, and there wasn't even a snicker. What in the world is going on?"

Not only did I not snicker, I hadn't even realized she'd turned the movie off and was staring at me.

"Nothing."

"Don't lie. Remember we don't lie to each other. Ever."

Well, she had me there. And I didn't want to lie to her. I didn't want to do this by myself, either. Not completely, anyway. The last two times I'd had Max to bounce ideas off of, but with him across the country, I might be able to call, but it wouldn't be the same as having someone right here with me.

Confess or lie anyway?

I chose confess.

"There's no way that guy died of a heart attack. It was murder."

"I knew it! I knew you weren't going to be able to let this go."

So good to know my friend knew me so well.

"It's not that I can't let it go."

She snorted, but I went on regardless. "It's that I

know what I saw. That was not a heart attack only. Something more is going on. I don't have a stake in this, but I don't like being told I'm wrong. Something is wrong with this Hammond guy and I want to know what. Why is he so sure it's a natural death?"

"Maybe you thought you saw more or imagined it after your fall?" She turned with her knee bent on the couch and a pillow tucked against her stomach.

"No, his neck was wrong. You don't break your neck falling on a bed after a heart attack." At least I didn't think so.

My cell rang on the end table. I checked the display before answering. It was a number I didn't recognize. That meant it wasn't Burton. Even if it was a telemarketer, I'd rather talk to them than continue listening to Gina telling me that maybe the doctor was right, or having Burton ream me out for chasing after something that hadn't happened.

"Hello?"

"I know I threatened to call the cops earlier, and I'm sorry."

It was the happy woman from St. James's office who had turned suspicious, though I couldn't blame her. I hadn't introduced myself and was asking some pointed questions about her employer. The kind that maybe someone from a bail bondsman's office might ask.

"Okay." What else was I supposed to say?

"I just wanted to tell you that I tried calling him several times and I can't find him anywhere. I did end up having to call the police and they said that I can't file a missing person report until someone finds his car in a wrong place or after three days."

"That is the law from what I understand." But why hadn't they told her he was dead? Unless I had imagined his face and it was someone else . . .

"But I'm supposed to get paid tomorrow!" she wailed through the phone, loud enough that Gina crept in closer and stuck her head against mine. "If I don't get paid, I can't pay my rent. And if I don't pay my rent I'm going to get kicked out and then what will I do with my baby dog? She can't live in a car! I can't live in a car!"

"No one is going to live in a car." Why on earth did I make that promise? I couldn't keep it, and if her landlord was going to throw her out on the first of the month for not paying her rent then he was either a jerk or she was way behind and he had just cause.

"It's not me I'm worried about, it's Peanut. She is a delicate flower and I can't do this to her."

"Okay, calm down."

Gina made a cutting motion at her throat. I knew what she was trying to tell me—no more promises, and I promised I wouldn't make any. "Where was the last place you remember your boss going?" I asked.

"Lunch. He was going to bring me back something because he wouldn't let me leave my desk in case an important call came in. But then he called to say he had an appointment and wouldn't be coming back after. I never did get lunch. I guess that's a good thing since I have no money to pay him anyway."

I had three quarters of a pizza left and maybe a chance to get some answers. Gina shook her head at me. I very deliberately ignored her.

"I can bring you some food if you think you might

have somewhere to start looking for your boss. I'm not an investigator or anything but I'm pretty good at finding people." Usually they were dead, but I wasn't going to tell her that. And it was possible this one was dead, too. I couldn't reconcile why the police wouldn't have told her that he was deceased instead of telling her they couldn't file a missing persons report.

With previous bodies, I'd been involved because I had something at stake: life the first time, my own; the second, Gina's. This time it was about justice. I might not be the best person, or even the most qualified person, to figure out what had happened. But at this point I felt like I might be the only person who cared that something bad had happened, especially since Hammond seemed determined to sweep it under the proverbial rug.

Something about the whole thing rubbed me wrong and I did not like being rubbed wrong—much like Mr. Fleefers, but with bigger stakes.

"Oh, would you? I live by the park. I'll be there in just a minute. I have to walk my little Peanut, and then I'll tell you anything you need to know. I tried to talk to the police, like I said, but they're telling me there's nothing they can do."

Maybe they couldn't do anything. I, however, could certainly try.

I got her address and hung up, then waited a minute to look at Gina. She wasn't going to be happy. The clanking of the dishes in the sink did not disabuse me of that notion.

When I looked up though, she was smiling. I'd

mistaken the sound for anger when apparently it was excitement to get out the door.

"So, does this mean I get to be in on this one? Last time I was the one under suspicion, so I couldn't do much. The time before that you didn't have any idea what was going on. This time I want in."

Whether or not it was my best idea, I was stuck with her. I filled her in on what little I remembered as we went to the apartment complex behind the park on the outskirts of town.

"And this Hammond didn't tell you who it was? It seems like a really big coincidence to me that the same guy you think is dead is also missing."

I didn't like coincidences. I shrugged and told Gina to flip on her turn signal to alert the jerk behind her that she'd be turning and he'd better slow down and get off our butt. Though her car was older, it was still worth a pretty penny if he rear-ended her.

She tapped her brakes a few times and he finally got the message, backing off just as she made the turn.

The address the woman had given us didn't actually show up in the apartments where I had assumed she lived. It hadn't sounded familiar. I directed Gina to drive behind the apartments and ended up on a small street with tiny one-bedroom houses. They used to be military housing for the inland naval base half a mile from us. And now they were all owned by my uncle on my dad's side. This woman wasn't going anywhere. If she could help me find my dead guy and prove Hammond was deliberately hiding something,

I might even be able to talk my uncle into letting her skip the back rent.

When I knocked on the door, I did not hear the yapping of a small dog. I very clearly heard the ferocious deep-chested bark of something much, much bigger.

I was a cat fan, witness Mr. Fleefers, and had met several dogs I liked, but they were always smaller, something I could tackle if necessary. I had thought about dog sitting or dog walking before the idea of cleaning came to me, but then I remembered that not all dogs were under ten pounds and decided I'd rather risk dishpan hands and squeaky shoes then get saddled with a dog who could literally drag me down the street.

The barking continued for another moment and then I heard the woman tell the dog to stop. Fortunately, it did. I only hoped she would give the down command before she opened the door.

She didn't.

Over one hundred pounds of brown and white dog came charging through the door as soon as she opened it just a wedge. Paws were on my shoulders and breath that stank of bacon treats hit my nose before I could hold my nose. Thank goodness it hadn't hit my wrist.

"Down, down!" the woman yelled. The dog paid her no mind and tried to lick my face over and over again. I turned my head back and forth to avoid the thing's tongue but it was no use. Gina stepped in at that point and scratched the dog's chest. It sat right down like she'd given it a command. How did she do that?

I wouldn't question the results. At least the furry

beast had sat his or her rump down on the floor and now maybe we could get to the reason we were here at all. My missing man who the police hadn't confirmed was dead.

"How long have you lived here?" I glanced around at the vast array of knickknacks and doodads, decorative dishes and crystal bells, china animals and an entire bookcase of tea sets. She hadn't moved in a month or so ago. Everything was covered in a fine layer of dust that my inner cleaning professional wanted to swipe away with a good feather duster if not actually take each piece down and douse it in soapy water. There was not a single piece of wall that wasn't covered by decorative plates emblazoned with Shirley Temple, Winnie-the-Pooh, and a variety of movie scenes from back in the day.

She was a collector. I hesitated to use the word "hoarder" because other than the dust, nothing was messy. There wasn't trash on the floor, no teetering stacks of old newspapers or magazines from decades ago. But she did have a lot of things. How did she keep them all with a dog this size in a house this small?

Again, that didn't have anything to do with the current situation. I needed info about her boss and then I needed to talk to my uncle and find out her situation and if he'd be willing to help her out.

First, though, I needed to find out her name. "I don't want to be rude, and I'm sorry if you told me already, but what's your name?"

She giggled, a high-pitched sound that set the dog off again. At least it stayed seated this time.

"I'm sorry I was so worried about my money, and

my boss, of course, that I totally forgot to introduce myself."

She giggled some more while I waited for her to actually spit out her name. Gina and I looked at each other, Gina lifting her eyebrow and one side of her mouth. Should I ask again? Would it not do me any good?

"And?" I asked after more giggling and more barking. I had to yell and that seemed to scare the dog enough to silence it. Peanut stopped before the owner.

"Oh, right. It's Marianne. Marianne Flotts. I moved here a few months ago from West Fairview to help out with Eli's business. I didn't like all the traffic and he found me this little house. I love it."

She'd only lived here a few months and yet she was already behind on her rent? That struck me as strange. I'd check with Uncle Barry, anyway, about the back rent.

"Maybe I can ask the landlord to give you a few days to come up with the money if you want. I know a lot of people in town and think I know the guy who owns these." I could have practically guaranteed that I could get a break on the rent, but I didn't want her to know it was my uncle. And how had she gotten so much dust in such a short time, unless she hadn't lifted a finger to clean since the day she'd moved in? Not my business. Well it was my business in that I cleaned, but I highly doubted she could afford my services, and I definitely wouldn't want to have to clean around a dog this big even once a month.

You could literally see the fur standing up off the couch. I'd hate to see what was under the 1970s water-wheel furniture. Probably more fur and maybe a few dust bunnies the size of Kansas from the dog I was pretty sure was a Saint Bernard. It was the same kind of dog that they used to put in cartoons as the rescue dog with a barrel of whiskey around its neck.

"Oh, that would be wonderful! I really need him to be found. Really. I have things due, along with bills and back rent, and he's the only one who can write the checks. I tried to get him to hire an accounting firm to do it or do direct deposit, but since it's just the two of us in the office, he didn't want to spend the money."

It made sense. I had thought about doing that for Letty but it was ridiculous if you have less than twenty-five employees.

"Is he usually good about signing the checks?"

She tilted her head and patted her hair. "For the most part, at least mine. Although not always everyone else's." She seemed to catch herself telling something she shouldn't have and clamped her lips together as she petted Peanut.

"Do you have anywhere that we might be able to start?" I asked to change the subject. This was why we were here, not for me to gauge how much it would cost for her to have me come in and clean, or to figure out why she owed back rent in just a few months of being here.

"The last place I remember him going to was the grocery store down the road. He was supposed to get subs and then come back. He called after an hour and said he had an appointment he had forgotten to tell me about."

"What kind of appointment? Doesn't Eli cover quite a few different aspects of the business world?"

She shrugged "Not that I know of. He pretty much only does the code inspections. He's so busy with those that he wouldn't have time for anything else."

I wasn't so sure I believed that. And why would she have thought I was hunting him down for something earlier?

"When you and I talked on the phone you said something about people harassing him. Do you think someone could have kidnapped him?" I wasn't going all the way to the killing thing just yet because I didn't want her to freak out even more about the money and stop thinking altogether.

I saw Gina open her mouth out of the corner of my eye and elbowed her. She got the hint and closed her lips, pressing them tightly together. I had a feeling I was going to hear about that later.

"I really don't know. He just seemed paranoid lately and a few callers really set him on edge. I heard him yelling at someone in his office telling them that they couldn't threaten him like that so I guess I thought someone was out for him."

"So, you never actually heard anyone threaten him? No one came in to the office as a threat?"

She shook her head and petted Peanut.

Well, there went that avenue, but it didn't mean it was a dead end. Pun not intended.

"Is there any way we could look in his office and maybe see if there was anything on his calendar or a note about where he went today?" I wondered if I was venturing into possibly bad territory but tried not to think about it. I'd be careful.

My hip had started hurting from standing in the doorway, and I refused to ask to sit down and possibly knock over any number of delicate things perched all over the place. I would ice the hip later when I was sitting down using any info Marianne gave me to find her boss.

"Oh, I don't know if I should do that." She bit her lip.

"It would be very helpful." Gina finally spoke up. "We could stop by my store, Bean There Done That, after to get a cup of coffee and talk about what you think might have happened."

The woman's eyes brightened. "I love that place. Best cinnamon buns ever. How do you make them?"

"Trade secret." Gina winked. "But maybe I could rustle one up for you after we visit the office."

Bribery, nicely done. I'd tell Gina that in the car. I had never really thought to do that myself, since you can't exactly bribe someone with a thorough house-cleaning and come out on top, at least not moneywise.

Peanut was taken into the back bedroom of the house and shut in. That must have been how the woman kept the house from being destroyed. I'd noticed when she opened the bedroom door that it was almost bare, like no-one-lived-there bare.

But then we were in the car. Marianne had decided to ride with us to save gas. It was about a mile to the office so I didn't know how much that saved her. Since I was getting access to the office without having to sneak in or manufacture an excuse, like offering up my cleaning services, I didn't mind her riding in the backseat. Although she did keep trying to lean forward between the seats, and that drove me crazy.

"Seatbelt," I said as we came to a stop sign. "We're not moving until you put it on."

"I can't. I don't like them. I feel trapped. What if we get into an accident and I'm locked into a burning car?"

I did everything I could not to roll my eyes. "Put it on or we're turning around and taking you back to your car."

I felt like a mom telling the kids I'm turning around if they don't knock it off. But Gina knew better and turned on the next street when Marianne sat back with her arms crossed over her chest and no seat belt on.

I fully intended to have Gina drop her off at her car in her driveway and wait for her to get in and follow us. Or we'd follow her. I was taking a gamble, but someone in the car without a seatbelt could get Gina a ticket. And if this woman wanted us to help her with her rent, she was not going to drive off in the wrong direction.

She huffed and puffed but finally gave in. We waited while she clicked her seatbelt into place with one final huff. Fine by me as long as it got done.

And then we were off. Who knew if we'd find anything, but I wasn't going to let anything slip past me. Not on my watch.

Chapter Five

Pulling up in front of the office of Eli St. James, I took a moment to run all the things I wanted to look for through my mind. There were of course secret journals, hidden doors, things taped to the bottom of drawers, safes, hidden pockets in books or shelves. I could be here for hours. But I was determined to do a thorough job. If Gina and I were truly the only ones looking, then I couldn't rely on luck.

All three of us got out of the car, Marianne stumbling out of the back. Gina didn't normally have more than two people in her car and I was never in the backseat so I forgot how much it could look like someone emerging from the womb when getting out. I did not laugh since that was inappropriate for the situation, but I did remind myself to never sit in the back. I'd probably have to be dragged out or at least rolled out.

We waited while Marianne dug into her enormous purse for her keys. I wondered if she called the cavernous bag something tiny and precious, too, but then decided not to ask because it didn't matter. She found the keys, unlocked the door, and darted into the office to shut off an alarm.

Good to know. Since the alarm had to be turned off it meant that no one was here. It might also mean that someone took the opportunity to kill Eli while he was out and about because the killer couldn't get to him here without detection. The more I tried to recall the face of the dead man on the bed the more I was sure that it had been Eli. I just couldn't figure out why the police would not tell his secretary that her boss was dead.

She flipped on several lights, and I wondered what it would look like from the outside. I wouldn't put it past someone from the police department to drive by just to see if I was snooping. I had a story all ready if they did.

I honestly hoped to not have to use it, but I'd learned by this point to have something ready so I wasn't caught off guard in my snooping.

I expected books and bookshelves, maybe some office furniture and potted plants, a few end tables, some magazines. Instead there was almost nothing. Marianne's desk was an old drafting table with no drawers at all. The walls had no pictures and not a single plant resided in the whole place. Through one door was a small bathroom that held nothing but toilet paper stacked on a shelf from what I could tell from here. Again, not a single drawer in the room.

The inner office wasn't much better. No bookshelves, no drawers. Where did the guy keep his files? *Did* he keep files?

I asked Marianne the last question, and she shrugged. "I just started a little bit ago and he told me he'd only been in this office for a few weeks before that. Said that we'd get to decorating once the money started flowing more. Since all of his jobs were on-site he didn't need a lot of extras in here." She shrugged again. "It was a job. I just wanted to start somewhere. I don't know that I was going to stay, but it got me here and in a house. That was enough for me."

Except that she was already late on her rent and was obsessed with knickknacks. I still didn't know why she'd come to this sleepy little town and decided more questions were in order. Something in her story didn't add up.

A knock on the front door stopped me from asking.

A shadow of a tall person loomed in the window, his uniform clear in the light of the outdoor fixture. At first I assumed it was Burton, then remembered he was on leave. It could be anyone really, but I just knew it was pointless to try and hide. I could have gone into the bathroom, but what was the point? I had my story, and I was sticking to it.

Marianne looked nervous opening the door. Why? Although a lot of people were nervous around cops, what did she have to worry about? Then again, a lot of people were nervous with the cops. And for what it was worth, even though I knew all of them, I still hesitated when I saw one, wondering if I'd done something wrong I didn't know about.

"Just let him in," I said. "He won't go away until you do." Folding my arms across my chest, I waited for Matt to come in with the newbie, Hammond, behind him. I had a feeling this was not going to be pleasant. I was not wrong.

"What are you doing here, and why are you doing

it with this woman?" Hammond asked several decibels above yelling.

At first, I wasn't sure who he was looking at. It could have been any of the three of us. But then he zeroed in on Gina and crossed his arms over his broad chest.

"What?" she said.

"Burton warned me about you getting into trouble. Your mother is apparently making him soup, or something, so I'm not supposed to arrest you. But don't push."

"Oh come on!" I said and had Hammond staring at me instead of Gina who was flaming red. I had no idea if it was rage or embarrassment, but this was not going to go any further. She was a grown woman, for God's sake, and did not need anyone telling on her to her mother. "We were asked by this woman to help find Eli because the police would not take a missing person's report. She grew concerned for his safety when he never came back with lunch."

Hammond's eyes narrowed, so I continued. At least he was staying silent.

"So, I see him dead and this lady says he's missing. Why didn't you tell her he was dead?" I crossed my arms and stared him down.

"We needed confirmation of his identity."

At the same time Marianne yelled, "You didn't say you thought he was dead! What about my check!"

Oh that was going to be a problem. I hadn't thought before I'd spoken. Something that wasn't completely out of character, and now I'd created more of an issue than I'd meant to. Story of my life.

And unfortunately this was not going to be the end. While Marianne caterwauled about all things money, Hammond looked me over and shook his head. I couldn't help what had happened. If he'd taken me seriously in the first place, we wouldn't even be here having this conversation. Maybe I should have just let it pass.

But I couldn't, and so here we were with a shrieking woman who now was going on about how was she going to feed her dog? Could I take the precious little thing for just a few days until she figured out her situation?

"No," I said. I didn't mean for it to come out so harsh, but Mr. Fleefers, my cat, would not take kindly to a huge dog like that living in the house with him, not to mention that I didn't have a house so much as a small studio apartment above my father's funeral home. To top it all off, there would be no room for me with a huge thing like that trotting around my considerably small space. I couldn't imagine how Marianne was able to move around in her tiny house, and I definitely wouldn't be able to do it in something half the size.

"Please!" She clasped her hands in front of her chest, her eyes pleading with me. No matter what she brought to the begging table, I was not going to be swayed.

"I'm sorry, but no, and neither can Gina. Maybe Hammond here could help you out. Unfortunately, it's not going to be me. I just don't have the room. Besides, like I told you, I know your landlord. I can work out the rent situation until we figure out what's going on."

"You're not figuring out anything." Hammond stepped into my space and put on a mad face.

I rolled my eyes before I could stop myself, and he growled. Well, he could growl all he wanted. I had committed myself to this now. "And are you going to look into this as a murder instead of your ridiculous claim that it was a heart attack?"

"It was a heart attack." His chin jutted out.

"And he just happened to break his neck on the way down to a bed on which he was perfectly positioned as if taking a nap?"

"I am not discussing this with you anymore. I will run a tight ship while Burton is gone. You will stay out of things and not concern yourself with anything that is not your business. Including this. We're trying to keep everyone we possibly can on the payroll. We shouldn't have to lay anyone off, so we can't be throwing around money on possibilities that have no basis in fact."

While partially that made sense, I felt like there was definitely enough to at least check a few avenues. Matt could do much of it right from his phone. But if Hammond wasn't going to try, then I wasn't going to stop trying.

"Then we have nothing more to talk about. If you go tattling to Mama Shirley then I'm sure I can come up with something that will equally get you into hot water. Think about it."

I should not have threatened him, especially since I didn't know him or how he would react, but I was pissed, really pissed and I was not going to be made to feel like an idiot and an imposter and a liar all in the same moment.

"Let's go, ladies." I picked up my purse and waited for Marianne and Gina to do the same thing. When they did we all looked at Hammond, waiting for him to leave first since he should not have been here and would in fact be going on his merry way to kick puppies or take candy from babies any minute now.

He grumbled but he still got moving. Then he sat in his car until we got into Gina's and drove off down the street. I didn't know if he'd been waiting to see if we'd go back in, or waiting for me to do something that would allow him to give me a ticket. I was doing neither.

If I needed to get back in, I had a key holder right where I could always find her. As for the ticket, I certainly didn't need one of those.

I very purposely asked Gina to stay exactly three miles under the speed limit going back into town and then out to Marianne's place. We dropped her off with my word that I would talk to the landlord and then we could go from there. I asked her to be available if I needed her and she agreed before being greeted with huge sloppy kisses by the little big Peanut.

"Well, that didn't go so well," Gina said from the driver's side.

"That's pretty much how it always goes. I try to figure stuff out and the police try to clam me up. But this one is much worse than Burton. At least with Burton I feel like I can make my way around him. This guy feels like the Great Wall of China, and he seems to be gunning for me."

"I should have my mom talk to Burton. Tell him to make this Hammond guy back off. You're like family, and Burton is family, so he should respect that."

I choked until I could clear my throat. "Uh, no, I don't think that's a good idea. The last thing I want is for your mother to get involved this early on." I'd asked her to help once when I had needed something specific to be spread around to everyone she knew, and she knew everyone. She was the absolute hub of all the gossip in our little town. But I had no intention of asking her to step between me and her cousin Burton.

"Well, this guy needs to back off if he's not going to do anything but wag his jaw at you," Gina said.

I laughed because I hadn't heard that phrase in forever. "He's not wagging his jaw. I get that he thinks I should keep my nose out, but I know what I saw, and I am not going to have people think I'm just trying to kick up a ruckus because I have nothing better to do. I spent so many years being vapid and having no purpose or anyone's respect. I won't go back there, Gina. And if one more person tells me to get a hobby I'm going to scream."

"You could always take up crocheting. I heard they have a great class over at the library."

I went to swat her and almost made her hit the curb. Sirens popped on behind us, and I closed my eyes. Just for a second, since I didn't want to be unaware if we hit anything else.

An hour and a tall whoopie pie latte later I finally got over being pissed at Matt for turning his lights on just to scare us. He was a pain in my backside, but he *was* able to tell me that Burton had sent him out to at least look around the outside of the office and make a few inquiries online. And he'd asked him to do it discreetly since he wasn't supposed to be working at all and didn't want Hammond to think he was interfering.

Still not the level of interest that a murder would have gotten, but it was something. And something was better than nothing. Or at least that was what I was telling myself at the moment, as I sipped and got ready to go home. Tomorrow I had to be ready to go to my other job at the funeral home across the street.

"I'm out." I finished off the last of the latte and licked my top lip to make sure there was no leftover whipped cream. I always had Mama Shirley pour it on thick because it was homemade and just this side of heaven. I might not sleep tonight from all the caffeine. It would be worth every ounce.

"What are you doing tomorrow?" Wiping down the counter, Gina tried to look busy. We hadn't seen Hammond coming in to tell on her, yet, but that didn't mean it couldn't happen at any minute. Perhaps he would think it would put a halt to us and our investigation. He would be sorely mistaken.

"I'm thinking research. I don't even know where to start. I guess we could look for license plates or any mentions of Eli. Kind of boring, and I have to work first. Mrs. Koser has her 'funeral' tomorrow." I did the air quotes because something like that deserved the air quotes.

"Ah, the spectacle."

"Yes, the one that's been in the making for nearly fifteen years."

"Well, have fun. Hopefully this one doesn't run longer than an hour."

"I'll call you as soon as I'm done."

"I can't wait to hear how it goes." Swiping at the counter, she laughed.

So did I. "Yeah, me neither."

The next morning, after a night filled with dreams of falling off that ladder over and over again, I was up and dressed in my black skirt with a jewel-toned shirt and low black heels. My hair was perfect and the "corpse" was in our best mahogany coffin directing the whole affair like she was making a movie.

"No, I don't want Jason to stand at my feet. He should be behind my head and his hands should be clasped at his waist, not behind his back. That looks too corporate, too uninviting. This should be a celebration, not a drill line!"

Sitting in the coffin with her arms propped on the closed bottom half, Henrietta Koser sounded just like a drill sergeant. I would have to look at the books over the last fifteen years, but I believed this was our nineteenth dress rehearsal for the day she would ultimately be laid to rest. I had a feeling some of the people in the room wished it would happen already so the show could get on the road.

She had everything planned down to the minutest of details. From where the tissues would go (tall ships on the boxes facing forward, not the flag) to the exact flowers, the punch that would be served, the music that would play at precise intervals, and where everyone would stand, and what expression should be on their faces. I had a feeling that when the actual thing happened this would all go to hell. It would be one big fiasco and then she would probably haunt us and them for the rest of our lives. In the meantime, it kept her content. And she paid for the rental of the funeral home every single time. Who was I to complain? Especially since I figured that by the time she actually died I did not plan on living here, or working here, for that matter.

"I want Tallie front and center, and, dear, I'd like you in the peach shirt you wore last time. It goes better with my flowers. I see you put a little weight on so you'll need to lose that, too. I don't want those thighs bumping into anything or making pantyhose noises when you're walking. That will mess with my music."

I looked at my dad simply to not look at her and spew out what I wanted to say. He gave a small shake of his head to tell me not to start anything, but it was close. However, I remembered that this family was well-connected in the area and were also not only house flippers but landlords. Could one of them know Eli? Did one of them know him better than anyone else? They had to do business with him. There weren't too many code enforcement guys in the area, and if they sold houses they had to have someone inspect them for any construction upgrades.

I zeroed in on Mrs. Koser's granddaughter, Taylor, who was my age. We'd gone to school together, and while she'd never been overly friendly to me, she had never completely been mean. Plus she was not someone I had turned my back on when I was Mrs. Walden Phillips III, so there wasn't that history to overcome, either.

Sidling up to her, I said, "Have you been to every one of these rehearsals?"

Mrs. Koser was still giving out strict orders to my father, who was dutifully writing them down on his clipboard. More power to him.

"Fortunately, I was able to avoid one when I was a freshman in college. She scheduled it while I was studying abroad. After that, though, she made sure it was a day when everyone was here and has since made it a stipulation of being named in the will. You aren't here, you get nothing."

Mrs. Koser must have had a lot of something since everyone always showed up.

"No talking!" she yelled from her place in the casket. It was both horrifying and hilarious to see her in there. We already had her obituary that she wrote herself on file, and the various places to send it along with a list of the types of funeral sprays each family member was supposed to buy. Nothing under seventy-five dollars.

Taylor pressed her lips together and took a small step back and then another. I covered her by stepping in front. Mrs. Koser's attention was focused on her son Tom and her instructions for him as to how he was to carry her. One year she'd made them carry her out to the hearse as pallbearers, but my dad put the kibosh on that after they almost dropped her. The last thing we needed was for someone to actually die at the funeral home. Bringing them here after the fatal moment was fine, but we did not want to be around for the during.

Taylor took another step back, and I stepped with her. Once she was behind a fake tree she whispered,

"Is there any way you could get your father to tell her she can't do this anymore? She's not dying anytime soon and this is not only morbid but ridiculous."

I didn't doubt nearly everyone in the room, including the staff, found that to be very true. But if ever there was a business where the customer was always right, we were it. My dad had tried to talk her out of it at first, had even charged her the second time she did it in hopes that would deter her, but nothing did.

"I'm sorry but no. He has to do what she asks, and she always asks nicely. It's only once she's here that she turns into a drill sergeant."

"I prefer to think of her as a banshee that won't go away."

An image of Mrs. Koser flying around in a ragged white dress howling down a lane popped into my head, and I snickered. Which was a major no-no in the funeral home world and got me the hairy eyeball from my dad. I mouthed "sorry." He just shook his head at me, and I knew I was going to be getting a talking-to before the morning was over.

"If you could put in a word for all of us letting him know that we think this is a waste I'd appreciate it."

"I can try but I don't think anything will change."

"That wouldn't surprise me, but at least if he tells her that her family might not be comfortable, then it's not coming from us."

Ah, the old passive-aggressive, make someone else take the fall move. Nicely done.

I'd used it a few times myself.

"Tallie, what are you doing over behind the bush? I need you in place. You, too, Taylor."

Chapter Six

We both jumped to, as if being given orders in the military. Mrs. Koser smiled. "Everything is perfect. Thank you so much for being here, everyone. Next year, if I make it, then."

A collective sigh was released. I didn't know if it was because they could leave or because they knew they'd all be back here again next year.

Dad helped her out of the coffin without wrinkling her perfect dress. Mrs. Koser smiled, again, showing her pearly white dentures, and thanked him while handing him a check.

"I'll call you with the date, Bud. I so appreciate the time and energy you put into humoring an old woman."

For my dad's part, he was genuine when he smiled at her and let her buss him on the cheek. He shot daggers at me, though. That lecture was not far off, dammit.

Just to hold it off a little longer, I went to shake Mrs. Koser's hand and give her my warm regards. It was what I was supposed to do anyway, and maybe it would go a long way to shortening that lecture.

"Tallie, just the girl I wanted to talk to." Mrs. Koser sank her fingernails into my arm.

"Uh, okay."

"We need to talk about this man you're hunting for."

My dad's eyes narrowed.

"Let's move this out into the hallway, ma'am, so that the cleanup can begin. It was such a wonderful presentation. I think everyone was pleased to see how lovely it will be." As I talked, I quickly moved Mrs. Koser into the next parlor and closed the door.

I didn't lock it, but I figured my dad would have his hands full with everyone else and wouldn't have time at the moment to follow me.

"I take it your dad doesn't know what you're doing, young lady."

Own up or bluff? This was Mrs. Koser. Owning up would go a whole lot further than trying to lie to the eagle-eyed woman. "He doesn't know and actually he's forbidden it in the past."

"If I could forbid it, I would, too. I've heard about your escapades before but this one is different. That man was bad business. Very bad business. He was bad business before when he was a home inspector with his reports but he was even worse once he became a code enforcer. I don't have my hand in much of our housing turnover anymore, but I know that he was trying to get my Larry to give him far more money than was quoted to not report a leak in the roof. Larry chose to fix it because he's my good boy. And then that scum Eli asked for an audience with me, as if I would pay him to write things off. But when Eli came to my house, he didn't ask about the house, he asked about a child."

"A child?" The conversation to this point had just been confirmation of what I already knew, but this was something else altogether.

"Yes, the man had a set like you wouldn't believe."

I choked and she giggled. It was good to hear her laugh like a teenager.

"Oh, yes, he did and they were as brassy as Mary Beth Danner's hair after her appointment at the salon. He wanted to know what I had done with the child I'd had forty years ago and if I'd given him up for adoption. He seemed to be under the impression that I'd pay to keep that secret."

What to say to that? I couldn't believe she would give up a child when family was so important to her, and I was pretty sure I'd just seen her forty-year-old son, Brett, out in the room. She'd had ten children over twenty-five years.

"I almost clocked him with my cane. The wretched man." She giggled again.

"But why would he ask that. Isn't Brett that child?"

She touched a few of the plaques people could use for mausoleums and trailed her fingers over the necklaces you could have made out of a loved one's ashes. "Brett was one of two actually. I did have twins but only left the hospital with one of those babies. The other one never made it out. He died in my arms."

Now, I knew what to say to that. "I'm so sorry, Mrs. Koser. That must have been difficult. Then and now."

"With so many other children you would think I wouldn't miss him too much, but each one is special.

You should have some of your own to know exactly how special."

Ah, yeah, we needed to move away from this subject. "So was he trying to blackmail you?"

"He sure was. Said he was a private investigator and had a boy who wanted to know who his parents were and if I wanted to keep my secret I'd better pay up. Why he thought I'd have two sons and give one away secretly was beyond me, but he seemed desperate."

A sideline of private investigating with blackmail to supplement his blackmail income for home inspections? It seemed Eli earned very few honest dollars. Or at least he hadn't when he was alive. Where were those files? What did he have on people? Who was this kid? Was there really a kid? So many questions.

"Anyway, sweetie, I just wanted to let you know that there might be more people out there who weren't able to tell the truth so easily. I won't say anything to your dad about you looking into this, but I think next time I'd like you to negotiate a twenty percent discount on the room."

"Sure, sure," I said, only half hearing her. This opened up a whole new avenue. I had to share with Gina!

I walked Mrs. Koser out of the parlor and to the front door, giving her a hug when she left.

Finally, the debacle was over. Earlier, I'd asked Taylor if I could give her a call with my dad's answer. I might not need that now with this new information. However, it couldn't hurt to get more information on the housing side of Eli's business. And since I had not found a good time to ask Taylor about Eli, I thought that at least would be a good intro. I was thinking of how to organize all this information and where to go next when the dreaded lecture commenced.

Dad had caught me as I was trying to sneak upstairs and call Gina to come over. I wished we were near the kitchen instead of on my steps, because at least I could have snagged one of my mom's fabulous cookies to help the lecture go down. But it was not to be. He stopped me on the landing and I wasn't going anywhere until I acknowledged I had not done the right thing and promised not to do it again.

"Tallie, I need you to take things here seriously. I raised you better than this and you know the rules. Laughing in the parlor is forbidden unless it is a celebration of life, and even then that's only for the family, not the staff."

"Sorry. It won't happen again."

"See that it doesn't. I will say that apology is running thin. It's the exact same one you gave me the last three times I had to pull you aside."

"Then write me up or fire me. Your choice."

He huffed out a frustrated breath. "My choice would be for you to understand how wonderful it is here and actually become a part of it. I'm willing to make you a partner with your brother. There's no saying that he can be the only beneficiary. I'm trying to pull your other brother in, too. This place would benefit from being run by three people. Perhaps, then, others could have an actual life before they have to be a guest here."

It was the first time I'd ever heard my father talk about wanting to be able to spend time away from the funeral home. This had been his life for all his sixty years, and I truly believed that he would die here someday, probably while embalming someone else.

"You want a life?" I admit I was shocked and that probably didn't come out quite the way I wanted it to.

"Your mother does." He shook his head. "Don't get me started."

"Ah." And I left it at that because he was not going to give me anything else no matter what I said. Honestly, I didn't know if I wanted anything else, at the moment.

"Will you at least think about it?" he asked into the silence that hung between us.

I couldn't say no so I said yes, even though I'd thought about it for years in dread and paranoia and depression. Thought about how I might not be able to do anything else but deal with dead people all the time. Funny enough, I got involved with dead people, anyway. Go figure.

He smiled at me, a rare occurrence when I was dressed for work and so was he. "Thank you. It would mean the world to your mother and to me."

God, nothing like a huge guilt trip. But I would pretend to think about it and then, after a few days, I would tell him absolutely not, just like I always did. Until then I wanted to ask about Eli since Dad seemed to be in a giving mood.

"So, Dad, before you go."

He turned back at the doorway, and I almost lost my nerve. He smiled at me so I plunged in. "Have you heard anything more about Eli St. James?"

"No, not yet. We have his contract, so I think we'll get him soon since it was a simple heart attack. Why do you ask?" He peered at me, and I could almost see the gears spinning in his nearly bald head. "You are not looking into another murder mystery, Tallie."

He didn't ask it as a question, he said it as a fact. He had no idea how wrong he was. "I'm just asking a question."

"And I heard all about how you thought you saw someone murdered at the Crossing Bridge Inn. Let it go." Tucking his arms over his chest, he raised his eyebrows at me. Classic disapproving-dad-waiting-for-daughter-to-back-down.

"Have you ever seen someone die of a heart attack with their head almost turned the wrong way?" I asked. "I know what I saw. He was perfectly positioned on the bed. He did not fall and break his neck while having a heart attack and land so perfectly. No matter what anyone says about my head injury possibly messing with my recollection and making me hallucinate, I know what I saw and when I saw it."

He shook his head. "No, I'll tell you nothing about him. You need to find a hobby, honey. Maybe your mom could teach you how to make all those cookies you love or how to sew. You could make clothes or even jewelry. Your Aunt Margo makes lovely jewelry. I can call her for you."

"I don't want a hobby. I want the police to take this seriously. What if we have a serial killer running around? Could you just call the coroner and see what he has to say?"

Shaking his head, he patted my arm. "Let me call your aunt, sweetheart. She makes really nice pot-holders. You need to keep out of these things."

"No. It's fine. Thanks." And I stepped away because I was not going to lie and say I'd stop looking, but I obviously wasn't getting anywhere here either. Gina and I would just hunker down and do our thing on our own. Maybe I could solve this before Hammond realized what a jerk he was and got involved. Wouldn't that make him mad? And serve him right for not believing me.

Finally able to escape, I ran up the stairs to my apartment and changed into comfortable clothes. After checking Max's phone's location on a people tracker, just because I could and felt closer to him knowing where he was, I called him and asked him if he wanted to have face-to-face time. Maybe I'd get a glimpse of a palm tree in Hawaii.

"Hello, sweetie. Love you, but it's really early here, Tallie."

I looked at the clock and it was eleven. Oh right, the six-hour time difference, so five in the morning there, whoops. "Sorry. But I don't mind seeing you with bedhead. It's one of my favorite looks on you."

"My internet is not all it's cracked up to be over here, Tallie. Why don't we just use the phone and then when I'm somewhere better we can go the face-to-face route?"

"Okay." I was disappointed I could not see the face I adored, but it was something to talk to him.

"So, what are you doing? I hear you might need a hobby."

I did not realize that the grapevine extended all the way across the country and part of the ocean too. "And how did you hear that?"

"Your brother sent me a text."

He was a dead man. Jeremy was going to need to pick out his own box, and then I was going to put him in there. "I do not need a hobby, and I do not need my brother texting you things."

"Calm down now. He was joking. And he and I have been friends for years. It's only because you're his sister as well as my girlfriend that I get all the info. If you had just been his sister, then I might never have heard about any of it. Since you're also my girlfriend I get all the details."

"And do you believe him?" I asked, waiting to see which answer he'd choose and how I'd feel about it.

"I don't think you need a hobby, and if you think it was murder then I don't doubt you. But I would hope that you're going to just let the police take care of this one instead of trying to do the investigating yourself."

"The police aren't listening and think that if they can get the coroner to confirm the cause of death as a heart attack without looking into it, they won't have to do anything more. Burton is out of commission for a little while because of some injury, and the new officer in charge has decided that I am a partaker in 'shenanigans.'" I made the air quotes around the word even though Max couldn't see them. "And now my dad is telling me to leave it alone."

Max hummed on the phone. I didn't know whether or not to take that as an "I'm sorry" thing or an "I'm not sure I believe you either" thing. Because he was so far away and I didn't want to get into a fight over the phone, I let it go.

"Anyway, how are things?"

"So, you are going to get involved, and you are going to investigate on your own."

"I'd rather not talk about it if you don't believe

me." I huffed out a frustrated breath and plunked onto my couch.

"Tallie." He drew my name out on a long sigh. "It's not that I don't believe you. It's more that I want you to be careful. I'd like to come back to an alive girlfriend instead of a dead one."

If that wasn't the sweetest thing someone has ever said to me I didn't know what was. "Aw, you really do like me." I smiled when he laughed.

"Of course I do. I wouldn't be talking to you if I didn't. Now my day is just starting and I know yours is nearing the middle. Why don't you get some rest and just let the police do their thing. I'm sure they'll figure it out eventually like they always do. That way you're not in any danger."

Except if Hammond decided to do nothing and never looked into the death, then I would be seen as a liar. It wasn't the worst thing I'd ever been accused of, but it still made me grind my teeth.

"Have a good day, Mr. Taxinator. I'll talk to you tomorrow."

"You, too."

We hung up and then I sat on my couch with my phone in my hand for a minute. I hadn't actually lied. I hadn't told him I wouldn't look into it even though I also hadn't told him I would. Good enough for me and my conscience.

Next on my list of calls was Gina. "Come on over after you close. We're going to have to do this quietly because apparently no one believes me, and I am not going to go down like that."

* * *

Letty had told me she didn't need me for any of today's cleaning jobs. With nothing else on my list today, I had hours until Gina got off work. And since I wasn't supposed to do too much, I figured I should go pick up my car. I could also try to see if I could get a closer look at the room where Eli St. James had died—murder or natural was debatable—but he had definitely died in the room. There were bound to be clues that the police hadn't picked up since they believed it was natural and there was nothing to investigate. I knew differently. And I was going to prove it.

It wouldn't be easy, but I was determined to not feel like a fool. I refused to have any more people tell me my imagination was getting away from me, that I was looking for a murder because I had nothing better to do, or that I needed a freaking hobby.

My father drove me over to the inn. I wished it had been anyone else, but when I called all my other friends and family, no one else was available. I knew as soon as I got into the car that the three-mile drive was not going to be short.

"Tallie, put your seat belt on."

I paused in doing that very thing with the clip in my hand and looked at him in disbelief. He stared straight ahead.

I made sure the click was as loud as possible by scooching over on the seat so that none of my body was covering the noise. I even said, "Done and secured, Captain," just to get his goat.

He simply started the car and pulled out onto Main Street.

I braced myself for whatever he was going to lay down on me.

"Have you thought more about my request?" he asked, still looking straight ahead.

I had to roll back through several conversations to figure out what he was talking about. At first my head was stuck on the hobby thing, and I almost told him that I had a hobby, my boyfriend, but then I realized he was talking about the offer to be a joint owner of the funeral parlor.

I should have walked. It was only three miles. I would have been fine, I was sure of it.

"Um, I'm still running it through my brain," I said lamely, looking out the side window. Talk about *awkward*.

"It shouldn't be that hard. You're part of the family, the business is part of the family, and it's what you're meant to do. Your brother told me that he would love to have you on full-time and would be willing to share everything with you."

I barely kept myself from snorting. Yeah, now that my brother had Gina of course my dad would want help, and there was no way he'd actually treat me as an equal. I'd spent the last year as the lackey, and rising above that wouldn't be easy even if I was put on the sign out front—Graver and Sons and Daughter, or Graver and Daughter and Sons. That would be better but it would never happen. I just wasn't ready to dash my dad's dreams just yet.

"I need more time." Of course the light in front of us turned red. Dad slowed down and gripped the steering wheel so hard his knuckles turned white. In anger? Frustration?

"Tallie." He turned to me this time and I was struck

by the added lines around his eyes and mouth. Many were from laughing. He could be a funny guy and was my rock when it came to my mom sometimes, but his mouth was not currently sporting a smile. "Your mother would dearly like you to give this serious consideration. We knew when you married Walden that you would not be around much, and we made our peace with that. Now, we're both so thankful to have you back, under the roof where we spend so much time, and in our lives. We didn't see much of you for those years when you were married, and we missed you."

I was the one staring straight ahead now. My dad's normal MO lately had been to chastise me for not taking things seriously enough, or not having the proper reverence for his business. We hadn't talked about the time I'd been gone since I'd come back. We'd both avoided it like pros. But now I had heat behind my eyeballs and was afraid I might leak a tear or two. I saw the inn up the road and hoped we made it through the next light without stopping.

"Thank you." It was all I could think to say.

"Your mother loves you and so do I. We'd like you to be a part of the family in a way we thought had been lost when you said 'I do.'"

Okay, now he was laying the guilt on thick. I was positively smothering in the stuff.

"I get it, Dad, and I understand what you're asking for, but you have to understand that even before I married Waldo I'd had no intention of going into the family business. I don't think dead people are my thing."

He snorted. "And yet you keep finding them. And, in this case, trying to investigate a death the coroner has deemed a heart attack."

The coroner had signed off on a heart attack? Why and how with a broken neck? What the heck? I'd have to ask Matt, but right now I had this conversation to endure.

Except that I didn't because we turned onto the lane that led up to the inn. I couldn't get out of the car fast enough. In my haste, I forgot to unhook my seatbelt and nearly strangled myself. My dad unclipped it at my hip, and I stumbled out of the car. I straightened myself along with my clothes as I stood up. I could do this.

But I didn't. Instead I leaned back into the car with my arm braced on the top of the door. "I am thinking about it. I promise I'll let you know my decision. You'll be the third person I tell."

"I guess that's going to have to be enough."

Again with the staring out the windshield. Now I felt like crap. Nothing like family guilt, huh?

Fortunately, my cell rang in my pocket. I yanked it out and answered without looking to see who it was, not caring if it was a charity asking for my annual donation to the local fire station. But, no, it was Burton.

"Tallie, we need to talk."

I was not up for another discussion of my failings and faults. However, it did give me the perfect excuse to say goodbye to my father by simply waving and walking away from the car. I didn't want to exchange more words about how I was not going to fall in with the way he had planned out my life. I knew that the conversation was not over and wouldn't be even when I said no, but I was very much okay with putting it off right now.

"I'm here, we're talking," I said into the phone instead of hanging up, which believe me had been very tempting.

"Are you in a place where you can be overheard?"

I looked around the front yard and saw no one standing around or outdoors. A curtain twitched upstairs but that was about it. I had about two minutes before Rhoda came out to see who was on her property. Burton could have those two minutes.

"I suppose."

"I need you to be sure."

"Sure, then, yes. I'm standing in front of the inn where the fictitious murder happened, given that your coroner declared the cause of death to be a heart attack, even though the guy's neck was very obviously broken. I'm just here to get my car."

"And look around if you can get Rhoda to open the upstairs bedroom?"

I certainly wasn't going to admit that. So, I didn't say anything at all, content to let Burton lead the conversation, and say goodbye as soon as possible.

"Ah, so that's a yes."

Again, I would not say a word. I silently pleaded the fifth. That still counted, didn't it?

"Well, when you're there, make sure you look under the bed for any kind of weapon, like a garrote."

"I . . . What?" I'd been all ready to defend myself so I was having a very hard time believing this conversation. Did Burton just tell me to look for clues? I took the phone away from my ear and stared at it to make sure the number was right and Matt wasn't playing a trick on me. But no, it was definitely Burton. What the hell?

And that was exactly what I said to him.

Chapter Seven

Burton cleared his throat, which historically had been the preemptive strike right before I got my rear end handed to me for interfering. "Look, being on leave means I need ears and eyes on the ground. I don't think it was a heart attack, either."

I had to admit that I choked and then paused, trying to regain my composure. Was he saying what I thought he was saying? "So why not tell that to Hammond?"

More throat clearing. Was he also sick? "Well, see, Tallie, there's a problem with that."

I waited and waited, standing in the middle of Rhoda's driveway for him to say something more. When nothing else was forthcoming, I sighed. "What about Matt?" Why was I fighting this? I planned to look into it anyway and it sounded as if Burton was actually asking me to do just that. Why wasn't I jumping on this? Maybe it was the little devil on my shoulder telling me to wait for him to actually say the words.

After the last two run-ins with him, I wanted him to ask me, not hint about it.

"Matt is under Hammond's command at the moment. I don't want him to get in trouble."

"But it's okay for me to get in trouble?"

Another sigh. He was going to get the hiccups if he didn't start breathing normally. "Look, I'm supposed to be on leave, and Hammond has been gunning for my position for the last eighteen months. He stepped it up after you solved the last murder, calling me incompetent. Then, I got hurt chasing that maniac down the street. The mayor asked him if he wanted to fill in while I am convalescing. Of course he jumped at it and then it was a done deal."

"Lordy." I liked the mayor but had a feeling I would now be questioning his taste in people.

"I can't have him look better," Burton continued. "I can't have the guys on the force get into trouble when I'm not there. You, on the other hand, aren't in danger of that."

"He threatened to put me in jail," I said.

"I'll break you out," he answered quickly.

Now it was my turn to sigh. "You will not, because you won't be able to. But I'm doing this anyway, so I'll stop making you beg for it."

I was pretty sure he growled, but that wasn't my problem.

"Should we have code names?" I asked. "Am I supposed to check in with you on the hour or you'll call some other cop to check on my whereabouts?"

His laugh wasn't big, but it was definitely a laugh. "No, 007, just make sure you let me know if you find something. We can build a case and then you can present it to him in all its glory so he can know what it feels like to be outsmarted by an amateur."

"Amateur sleuth," I clarified.

This laugh was bigger and then he groaned. "I can't keep laughing, hurts my side. But fine, amateur sleuth. So, go check out the inn and let me know what you find. Be careful, though, and subtle. *Please.*"

"Will do, Bossman Burton."

He hung up laughing, and I wasn't sure what to do with that. We hadn't exactly been enemies before. We'd always been on the same side of justice, but we definitely had been at odds about how to get that justice. Now I was going to be reporting to him in his sickbed.

Wasn't life funny?

Shoving my phone into my back pocket, I looked at the inn from my vantage point. Someone had died here, someone had made that death happen with no thought of being caught. My mind zipped around with the possibilities. Who could it have been? The cars in the parking lot when I'd put my jacket away popped into my head. Had those people been helping or was one of them a killer? Rhoda hadn't mentioned anyone being there, not that she had to, but it was still curious.

At this point I was thinking she just hadn't known what was going on right under her nose. Maybe Eli invited someone here to have a conversation with them out of the public eye, maybe about finding that kid? And it went wrong. Then again, he may have wanted money and the killer had followed him here, then took the opportunity to kill him and leave him in a room to be found by yours truly.

Paul rounded the barn with a smile. Assessing him, I wondered if he could have done it. I quickly dismissed the possibility. Paul had been around for years and was one of the nicest, gentlest people I knew. He was in charge of the children when they had activities at the inn. His balloon animals were the best and he made balloon hats that even I wanted to wear. No way would he have used those hands to break someone's neck.

Paul waved and came over to where I was standing, still looking at the building and trying to think of what I was missing, or who could have done this.

"Afternoon, Tallie. What brings you out this way?" His dark hair waved back from his forehead, and his brown eyes smiled warmly.

"I'm here for my car. I left it in the lot after what happened yesterday."

Tucking his hands into the back pockets of his coveralls, he sighed. "It's a shame that the man had a heart attack here. I'm hoping this won't be bad for business."

"The police told you that? I'm not sure that's what happened."

"No? That's what the police said. Confirmed it with Rhoda this morning, and she feels so much better. A murder would be very bad business for the inn."

Was there a warning there? For me to back off? But he smiled at me, gentle eyes and all. I didn't feel threatened in the least.

"Oh, Paul, what are you doing taking up Tallie's time?" Annie swatted his arm good-naturedly as she walked up. Her hug was all-encompassing and comforting. "We heard you were doing better. That true?"

she asked me, stepping back and hooking arms with her husband then laying her head on his shoulder.

They were an adorable couple and had been around this area for years. I don't remember when they moved in, but it was long enough ago that I felt like they'd always been here.

"I do feel better. I'm here for my car."

"And she's not sure that the guy died naturally. What do you want to bet she's going to try to do that snooping around thing to outsmart the police?" Paul added and then laughed.

"Oh, Tallie, don't get yourself into this. It was a simple heart attack. Rhoda cried when the police told her that because it meant she didn't have to tell people that someone was killed here, or have it go on one of those rating sites." A few blond hairs escaped her bun in the light breeze. She tucked them back with a smile. "Now, why don't you go in to see Rhoda? I bet she has a muffin or two that you could take with you."

"Right, muffins. I love muffins." I was tired of trying to convince people I wasn't lying or making a big deal out of nothing. I would just have to be subtle like Burton had asked. My face must have given me away this time though; I'd have to work on that. After Annie lectured me of course.

Annie let her husband go to put her arm around my shoulders. "Sweetie, I know you like justice and you've been an amazing help to the police over the last year, but I really think this was just a simple death at the wrong place. Rhoda doesn't want to worry about an investigation. She's nervous and bereaved for the man himself, but also scared for her business."

I nodded at the two and slipped out from under Annie's arm. They were fiercely protective of their employer and I understood that. I would be fine with it being a natural death, too, since that would mean we did not have another killer on the loose. I couldn't let it go, though.

"Well, you guys have a good day. I'm going to say hi to Rhoda, then hit the road."

"Have a good day, sweetheart. And if you can get your man to come by, I'll be doing a Victorian carriage ride through the woods next month in the snow. I bet he'd love that, and we'd love to have you two."

I waved as I made my way toward the back door and the kitchen.

What was I going to say to Rhoda? If Burton and I, along with Gina, were the only ones who thought it was a suspicious death, and he hadn't seen anything since he was convalescing, then why was I continuing to pursue this? No, I didn't want a murderer running around, but maybe it was an accident. Maybe he really did die naturally. He could have hit his head on the fireplace mantel, wrenching his head around as he fell.

Rhoda came out just as I approached the door.

"Here for your car, sweetie?"

"Yes, and a muffin since I heard you're making them." I walked my fingers across the counter. "Did you have someone come in and clean the room where they found Eli? I could do that while I'm here. All my gear is in my car." Apparently, I was not yet ready to let it go, no matter what I told myself.

She frowned and placed a hand on my arm. "Oh, honey, thank you for the offer, but I've got it handled.

Since it was a heart attack and there's nothing more to it, I'm just going to spiff the place up myself. Go home and do something constructive with your time. Like make those babies your mama's always asking for."

"Uh, the boyfriend is across the country so I'm pretty sure that might be a little bit miraculous. And I really don't mind helping, Rhoda. I'm sure it would make you feel better to know that it's all cleaned up. You wouldn't have to lift a finger." I had to get her to let me into the room. How else would I do what Burton wanted me to?

"Maybe another time, honey. Besides, per that nice Chief Hammond, no one is allowed in that room right now, not even me. Sorry. But I do have some sticky buns you can take home with you."

"Thanks." I took a deep breath and plowed right in. "What was Eli even doing here? You said no one was on the property."

Her normally open, smiling face closed down and went blank. "I guess I forgot to mention it. Now go on with your sticky buns." She shoved the box into my hand and wasn't very subtle about shoving me back to the driveway.

"Oh, before I go, can I use the bathroom?" I was desperate for a chance to get in there and running out of ideas.

Without a word, she led me to the powder room under the stairs, then waited until I came out to hand me the sticky buns. Not good and totally not what I had wanted!

Burton was not going to be happy with my first three minutes on the job. Maybe I should have asked to use the bathroom upstairs. But I hadn't been quick enough and now I was standing by my car and out of excuses. No one should have been upstairs, much less a building inspector with no appointment. So why wasn't she protesting this more?

Right. Because she didn't want the bad publicity.

Was she really going to go with the party line and not admit that something bad had happened here? I guess we'd see.

I climbed into the Lexus and waved at Rhoda as I pulled around the circle to leave. She stood in the doorway the entire time as if guarding the house. Or was she guarding a secret?

"I brought wine and cheese." Gina let herself into my apartment. Mr. Fleefers immediately wound his way through her legs. He never did that for me. In fact, I hadn't even seen him since I'd been home, and then he appeared magically when Gina waltzed through the door.

The sticky buns were long gone, and I hadn't come up with a better way to tell Burton that I'd failed than to just say it fast, like taking off a strip of wax on my upper lip. He had sounded resigned but not necessarily angry, so I took that as a good sign and promised to do better next time.

Taking the bottle of wine and the little container of cheese, I let Gina and the cat have their love affair while I put everything out. I had a file folder, a highlighter, and the printer set up. I didn't know what I thought I was going to do with all this, or why I felt the need to act as if I was running an agency of some sort, but since no one except Gina, and now Burton, believed me, I was going to keep an accurate trail. Then, I was going to rub it in all of their faces when I knew who did it and why. Well, everyone except Rhoda, Arthur, Paul, and Annie. They just wanted their business to not suffer. I understood that, but I couldn't sweep this under the rug any more than I'd sweep real dust under a rug.

"If you're finished messing with my cat, I'd like to get down to business. You have work tomorrow and so do I." With four houses to clean on the schedule, I couldn't cancel. Fortunately, Letty was taking them because of my wrist, but I'd agreed to come along and help with some of the lighter stuff. There was also another funeral tomorrow. This one for a young teenager, which meant far more mental preparation than when the person had made it to a ripe old age and had lived every day to the fullest.

I wasn't going to think about that right now, though, because it would make me sad. I needed to hold onto my mad so that I could at least get a jumping off point.

"Mr. Fleefers still not hanging out with you?" Gina asked, carrying the cat draped over her shoulders. That was going too far.

I stuck my tongue out at the cat and he hissed at me. "Fine, let's see where your next can of food comes from, the discount store or the grocery store."

"Aw, don't listen to her, my pretty. If she doesn't get you good food, I will." She stroked the cat, who of course purred for her.

"Traitors, both of you."

"But we both love you, don't we, baby?" The cat rubbed his head against Gina's cheek but kept his eyes narrowed in my direction.

"Anyway!" I set the laptop on the kitchen table and pulled up two chairs. "Did you bring your laptop?"

"Actually, I brought a tablet and figured I could email you the links to anything I find important. I wasn't lugging the laptop over. That thing is ten years old."

"You know getting a brand-new one would be a business expense."

"And one I'm not willing to pay for since I have my eye on this new espresso machine." She sat in one chair while I pulled up the other to the table.

"Make Jeremy buy it for you. Aren't you coming up on some kind of anniversary? I know, you could make one up! He probably wouldn't even know."

She laughed, but then sighed. "No, no anniversaries yet. I don't know if we'll have one. Your brother is a hard fish to keep caught."

I really didn't know if I wanted to hear this, since it was my brother, but she was also my best friend, and we'd always shared everything. "What's going on?"

"Oh, he won't even consider moving in together until some future date when we may, or may not, be married. Apparently, it would look bad for the local funeral home director to be sleeping with someone who isn't married in the eyes of the church."

I nearly choked on my small glass of wine. "He said that to you? And how is that any different from walking over to your house and then hoping he leaves before anyone sees him in the morning? With this town, he has to understand that people know you're sleeping together, and it's none of anyone's business anyway."

"Well, I guess different enough according to him. He doesn't want to sneak anymore. He thinks we should get married. And to be honest, I'm not even sure I want to ever be married." She held Mr. Fleefers's face to hers. "I saw my parents' marriage dissolve, and your marriage, even though it was from the outside. Maybe it's just not worth it."

I'd been thinking the same thing with Max, but hearing the words come out of her mouth automatically made me into the devil's advocate. "But it can be awesome, and then you'd really be my sister in name and in my heart." My brain kicked into gear. "Wait, did he propose?"

It might be a little early for that, and I was pretty sure Gina would have told me as soon as it happened, but you never know if you don't ask.

She sighed. "No, he didn't propose, but he did give some speech about neither of us getting younger, and maybe it's something we should think about."

Not nearly as romantic as Max wanting to come home to an alive girlfriend, but we couldn't all have the perfect mate. "Meh, let him twirl for a little bit until he realizes that he might not want to make it sound like a last-resort kind of thing."

Laughter poured out of her, and I joined her.

"So, let's start looking," I said. "I hope that tablet's ready for some serious sleuthing."

"You know it is. Thanks for letting me in on this one, Tallie. I really want to bring it home to Hammond. He is a jerk. By extension, we should show up

Burton, too, since he seems to think that we're stupid, especially since previously he's threatened to tell on me to my mom."

I had a feeling that was the reason why she wanted to do this, other than just not wanting to be left out. "We're not going to be able to show Burton up this time." I avoided her eyes for the moment.

"What? Why?"

"Well, first of all, he's on leave. I'm surprised your mom didn't tell you that."

"She might have," Gina admitted. "I don't always listen to everything she says or I'd never get anything done between recaps of her daytime television shows and local gossip."

"Well, Burton called and asked me to look into it. Said that he needs eyes on the ground and can't ask any of the people in the department because he doesn't want them to get in trouble." Now I looked at her and found her dander fluffed to the fullest.

"Are you kidding me? After everything he's blamed and shamed you for, now he wants you to sleuth against the police for him? Ridiculous."

"I partially agree, but it's at least good to know that we aren't the only ones who have questions about Eli's death. I said I'd help. Especially because Burton said that Hammond wants to replace him permanently as our chief of police. Hammond called him incompetent."

"How dare he? That's my family he's talking about. Oh, now we're going to hand this to Hammond on a silver platter polished to a shine so bright he'll go blind."

That was my girl. I figured having someone trying

to blacklist a family member would get her to agree. And it worked.

"All right. Here's the plan. You look for stories about things Eli St. James might have done criminally. I'll look for background information on him."

We both hunkered down over our machines and went to work. A few times she made a noise like she'd found something, but when I asked she said it was nothing. After an hour, all the cheese and wine were gone. We looked at each other and shrugged.

"Nothing," she said. "How can there be nothing when Marianne said that people were after him? Wouldn't he at least have some kind of rap sheet? Or complaints if it had to do with his business dealings?"

I shrugged again. "Maybe not. There was the whole Darla thing where her true name wasn't known and all the blackmail was under the table and behind people's backs. There was nothing on her until we got to the point where we knew who it was. I guess it could all just be verbal threats." Though in this age of social media, there was usually something on the internet. This guy had very little. A social media page and an old website from when he had been a home inspector before, but that was it.

"Is this how it always is?" She frowned, tapping her fingers on the table. "I really had this thought that we were going to be like Nancy Drew or Scooby-Doo. Out finding clues and piecing them together. Making everything all right without a second of downtime."

I laughed because that was so not how this worked. And normally Burton was far more vocal about me staying out of things, but then again normally he was on the case trying to solve it. Maybe he didn't always tolerate me, but he wasn't as mean as this Hammond guy.

"I don't know about Scooby-Doo and the man in the mask, but I do know that it's not all chasing around in the Mystery Machine." I smiled. "Go home, we'll see if we can find anything tomorrow. Matt said that Burton asked him to look through a few things, so there's a possibility that we really can just sit back and watch it unfold. Don't mention Matt's involvement to anyone, though, because Burton says it could be seen as stepping on toes if we're mucking around while Burton's on leave."

"Oh, and if we keep it quiet, maybe he would owe us one," she said gleefully, bouncing in her chair.

I laughed because I doubted that. On the other hand, I guess it could be true. I wouldn't mind one bit having Burton owe me.

"Besides, you don't believe that you'll actually just sit back and watch it unfold." She picked up Mr. Fleefers, who'd jumped off her lap when she started bouncing. "Tell me honestly that you don't like the thrill of the chase, the adrenaline of finding things out before Burton. You love it, don't lie."

I thought for a second. Surprisingly, I had never really considered that. The first time I'd solved a murder I was trying to save my own life and find the money to save my finances. I just happened to be in the wrong place at the wrong time in several scenarios. The second time they were trying to place the blame on my best friend for a murder she didn't commit. Since I couldn't let them do that, I'd stepped in. I didn't think I did this just to be nosy, though there was definitely a Sherlock Holmes element where

I wanted to know the facts. Maybe I really did need a hobby.

I shut that thought down before it left my mouth. This was not about sticking my nose in where it didn't belong. This was about finding out who that murdered man lying on a bed at the inn truly was. And I was simply making sure that whoever had done it got their justice.

With that in my mind I said, "I'm not about besting Burton, I'm about justice."

She giggled. "Like a superhero. Should we get you a code name? A mask? Oh, a cape!"

I rolled my eyes and threw a pillow at her. "I think we're done for the night. Why don't you go home? Go ahead and dream about being Nancy Drew or Daphne, whichever works for you. Then you can call me in the morning and tell me where the body is so we can get started unmasking the villain."

Gina hugged the pillow to her chest. "Should I tell your brother I'm helping you before he finds out from someone else? He's not going to be happy, is he?"

I scoffed, because, really, what else was there to do? Again, she was a grown woman and didn't need anyone's permission. I'd told Max I was looking into this, and he hadn't told me anything I wasn't expecting. I chose to ignore him. Well, I hadn't told him, exactly, but I hadn't agreed to stay out of it either. It was a gray area, I admit, but I was sticking to it.

"It's totally up to you," I answered. "He's probably going to have a problem with it, so you might want to consider whether or not it's worth fighting about."

She closed her eyes. "I believe you, and I want to help, though I'm glad I wasn't the one who found the body. One dead body at the bottom of my staircase is enough for a lifetime. I want to help you, though."

"Then tell him." I shrugged. "What's he going to do? Cut you off? You're old enough to make your own decisions."

She bit her lips and crushed the pillow. "I'll tell him tomorrow. Maybe if I have that dream, and we solve it tomorrow, I can tell him after the fact."

Gina was still laughing on her way out the door, but I was feeling the pressure. She was going to be whipping me along like a trick pony, and I hoped she wouldn't be too disappointed if it took longer or if it wasn't easily solved.

My gut was telling me differently. And I trusted my gut. At least about this.

Chapter Eight

With Gina gone, I glanced at the clock. Still early enough to place that call to Taylor, Mrs. Koser's niece, and see if she knew anything more about fixing the inspections reports. While I believed Mrs. Koser about Eli trying to ask her about a baby, I had no way of researching that. Eli hadn't shown up under any listings for private eyes and I had a feeling it was a word-of-mouth thing that no one was going to want to confirm.

"Hello?"

"Taylor, hi, Tallie here."

"Oh, man, did you get your dad to tell Grandma that she has to stop these funeral home rehearsals?"

Oops, I hadn't even brought up the subject, but I knew exactly what my father would say so I just channeled him.

"Unfortunately, there's nothing we can do. I did ask him to talk to Mrs. Koser, but I don't believe it will do any good. Sorry about that."

She sighed. "No, it's okay. It was at least worth a try."

I scribbled a note to myself to actually ask my father about it tomorrow.

"Well, thanks, anyway, Tallie. I appreciate the call."

"Wait. While I have you on the phone, I wanted to ask about Eli St. James."

"Why? What do you want to know? He's dead, we're all happy and might actually get fair assessments without him reaching out his greedy paws. I'm fine with that."

Would she have done it and was trying to cover up for herself? I doubted it. "So, do you think it was a murder?"

"I don't really care either way. I'm just glad he's dead. We had to pay a pretty penny to get him to assess our last house fairly. I went after his brother, but that guy's a jerk. He pretended he had no knowledge of previous issues and no matter how much I searched I couldn't find any evidence of past complaints. Some people dropped their complaints when they got what they wanted anyway. If any did make it to his office, I guarantee they went in the shredder."

"Then you don't know who might have had a grudge against him?"

"The list of those *without* a grudge would be shorter. But, no, I have no idea who would have hated him enough to kill him. Sorry I couldn't be more help."

"That's okay. I appreciate your time. And if my dad can get your grandmother to change her mind, I'll let you know."

We hung up and my shoulders slumped. Where to go next?

I said good night to Mr. Fleefers, who lifted his tail to me as he strolled away. After turning out the lights,

I laid there and couldn't get the image of Eli lying on the bed with his eyes wide open out of my head. How long had I been out after my fall? Would someone have known that I saw the dead body before I woke up yelling about it? Who had closed the door to the room just as I squeegeed that last spot?

Someone had closed the door! How had I not remembered that sooner? With the fall and the police and the dead guy I had completely forgotten! Glancing out my front window, I looked across the street to find Gina's apartment dark. Dang it! I made another note to myself to tell Gina tomorrow.

I ran through the scenarios of how I had fallen off the ladder and couldn't come up with anything. It was simply gravity that had messed with me and the ladder. No one had been below me, so they didn't tip the ladder over.

Or had they?

As my eyelids finally drifted shut I thought about that possibility. Had someone tipped the ladder after they'd killed the guy, thinking I'd seen something? Killing two birds in one day? But I'd been lying on the ground for at least a few minutes, from what I understood, and the killer could have finished the job before Rhoda hit me with the bucket of dirty water. If the killer had done that, I wouldn't currently be lying in my bed wishing Max was next to me so I could talk this through with him.

Finally, I slept. In my dreams, I was the one who was racing around in the Mystery Machine with my faithful dog looking at mask after mask.

* * *

I didn't get the best night's sleep, to say the least. That only really happened when Max was here. But I did have a ton of dreams that I remembered and was trying hard to sort through. I didn't know what many of them meant. I considered asking Ms. Beatrice, our local tarot card reader and palm reader, but I hadn't visited her in years. The last time, I had wanted to know if I'd truly made a horrendous mistake in marrying Waldo, my nickname for my husband, which he hated when he was alive.

She'd said absolutely, and I still hadn't believed her until I found out he was a cheating jerk, both in the bedroom and with money.

I didn't need her, though. It was probably just my imagination working overtime, trying to figure out how I could have seen Eli as no one else had.

Who had been leaving the room when I'd fallen off the ladder? Someone had closed the door, but no one except Rhoda and Arthur had been in the inn, according to Rhoda. Then again, she'd downplayed that Eli had been there, even though she'd been shocked when I had told her someone was inside one of the inn's rooms. Was that why Rhoda didn't want me in the room? Had the police truly closed it off? Where would she put whatever guest had booked it for the weekend? If it was ruled a natural death, then she didn't have to tell anyone and could keep all her reservations. And it was only Wednesday so they still had time to clean everything up.

Rhoda had said they were going to be full this weekend so guests would have to stay in that room. Would she tell them a man had died there only days before they opened up their suitcases and settled in for a vacation?

My alarm rang, letting me know I had to get moving. I would think more about it later. Right now, I had to help Letty clean our first house of the day.

Driving to the Rockwells', I enjoyed the breeze coming in the rolled-down window and sang along to the radio to distract myself.

A thought had been running through my gray matter ever since I'd picked up my car, and I desperately wanted it to go away. Maybe Rhoda wanted it to be a heart attack to cover up the fact that she'd killed him. She'd thought I was gone until I screamed. Maybe Arthur had called to her for something after she killed Eli and she had closed the door figuring she could come back and clean up the room after she'd dealt with Arthur. No one else should have been in the house, and she thought I was no longer on the property, so it would have been the perfect crime.

But I couldn't imagine Rhoda killing anyone, especially not by breaking a neck. I would have considered Arthur as a suspect first. Except Arthur was rolling around in a wheelchair, so how would he have been able to reach up and do that, then lay the body out on the bed so perfectly? And the person I saw close the door was walking.

I had heard cars pulling up in the drive when I was up on the ladder. Maybe Eli had agreed to meet someone at the inn and things had gone downhill fast from there. But wouldn't Rhoda have known he was there? She had seemed as surprised as I had to hear that he was in her inn. Had she faked that surprise?

I needed to let this go until I finished with the first house.

For the most part, things were right in my world for the first time in a long time, and I tried hard to be thankful for that every day. I had a roof over my head, one I didn't have to scream in unless I was watching a particularly scary movie or was trying to wax my legs on my own. I had a car that worked, parents who could be a pain but loved me. Siblings who were also a pain—I sensed a theme here—but they also loved me as I loved them. Good friends. And Max.

The glow I got from just thinking his name made me hesitate, but I went with it. He was good to me and for me, and I couldn't wait to see him again.

There, I thought it and meant it. If that made me a little nervous, then maybe it was actually meant to be this time. I'd run away from life with Waldo to escape the path I thought I had to go down. This time I was choosing to make my own path.

All the money from Waldo's secret stash was gone and I was working both my jobs to make ends meet, but I didn't mind. It was honest work, and that was also good.

Pulling up at the Rockwells', I was surprised to see that Letty hadn't shown up yet. I couldn't clean by myself. I'd agreed to meet her to help with some of the more minor things since I had asked her to pretty much take all my jobs and keep up with her own. We'd moved a few but not many since Letty was excited to have the extra money.

I wished there was more I could do for her, but I still had to work the jobs, too.

My phone rang in the cup holder between the

seats. I glanced at the screen and saw "Chief Eek"—
my nickname for Burton. I hoped he never saw that,
but it often made me giggle. Not today. If he was going
to tell me I wasn't working fast enough, then I didn't
want to hear it.

Since I had a few minutes before Letty showed up
and got her things out of her car, I decided to answer.
It wouldn't be better to leave him hanging. He'd just
call back until I answered, leaving stoic messages
to call him right away. It was a pattern.

There were a lot of patterns in my life. Some I
needed to break, but some I kept because they were
too good.

"What?" I was not nice when I answered the phone.
I wasn't feeling nice at the moment.

"What are you doing, Tallie?"

"Should you even be asking me that since you're on
administrative leave? I thought you were out for the
next six weeks." I could be snooty too.

He sighed, and I imagined him pinching the bridge
of his nose. "Tallie."

"Burton."

"Look, don't get me started. Things are about to go
to hell at the station. Hammond is pulling out all the
stops to make as many changes as he can while I'm
not there. I know you're not exactly a pro at this, but
I need info. You're the only one I can trust to get it for
me. I need you to look around and use that incredible
sniffer you have to seek out clues about who killed Eli
and why Hammond isn't taking this as more than a
health-related death."

I sat stunned in my cushy front seat. I didn't even
know how to respond to that. Not only was he asking

me to help when normally he was yelling at me to keep my sniffer out, but he'd also given me a compliment. I wasn't sure what to do with that.

"Did you hear me?" he asked.

That I could answer. "Yes, I did, and I appreciate you asking, and for the compliment, but I can only do so much and so fast. I did think of something last night."

He waited, the silence vibrating across the connection. I finally sucked it up and carried on.

"What if I'm wrong? What if he really did just die? What if I'm making too much out of this? I haven't been able to find anything." And I was not ready to tell him about only Rhoda being mobile and in the house and someone closing the door as I got a good look at Eli St. James. That was speculation. I was not going to ruin the life of a dear friend when I didn't have the facts, or even a solid motive.

I kept the info about Eli blackmailing, or trying to blackmail, Mrs. Koser, to myself. Forty-year-old babies that she obviously felt weren't a secret probably didn't matter. Her claim that he had been blackmailing her, though, might need to be taken with a grain of salt, considering it came from a drama queen who'd been practicing her own funeral for fifteen years.

"Don't flake out on me now. You might not have anyone involved with this dead body in this instance— they don't think it was you, and I'm not looking into any of your friends. But if someone killed Eli, then we have to know who. I can't do anything about it. I need you to dive in like you've done before, only this time you're helping me instead of working against me.

Somehow Hammond got Doc Jerome to sign off on a death without checking the deceased fully. Even Matt said that the guy's neck looked wrong, but when he tried to put it in his report Hammond shut him down."

"Isn't that illegal?" Oh, now, we might be getting somewhere.

More sighing. Were breathing exercises part of his rehabilitation program? If not, they should be.

"Only if I can prove it," he said.

And there was the crux of the situation. My clues often came to me through sticky fingers and some not-so-legal practices. Normally, I had no fear, but if Burton was going to try to build a case, then he would need legitimate stuff. That I didn't know if I could supply.

I told him as much, and he laughed.

"Just go about it as you have in the past. I'll make sure it looks pristine while coming from the right channels. You have a vivid imagination. Use it to get creative."

No, I didn't, and told him as much. "I can't even draw a stick figure. I failed every creative-writing anything I ever took. I looked at the facts and went with what happened just like I've done the other two times. And isn't falsifying where things came from illegal, too?"

"Not if I do it right. This is my job on the line and my town, Tallie. I want to keep it safe. Something about Hammond puts my antenna on full alert."

We said goodbye, and I sat for a moment, not sure what to do. This was a whole new game. It was my town, too, and if Hammond was dirty, I wanted him gone. Matt could step in for the moment, if need be, or Burton could get back early from leave. In the meantime, I guess the whole thing was up to me and my sidekick, Daphne/Gina. I texted her to let her know we'd talk later. Within seconds, she sent me back a smiley face. At least it wasn't a string of strange emojis like she sent when talking about my brother.

Letty fortunately pulled up at that moment and took me out of thinking and into action.

"Hey, boss, you sure you want to do this? I really can handle it on my own." She pulled the vacuum cleaner from the back of her little hatchback and a bucket full of supplies. She was a hard worker, and I was more than happy to have her on my team. I didn't even make money off her jobs, to be honest, but she didn't want to be her own boss. So, I paid her what I got minus taxes. It worked for both of us.

Previously I had left all the taxes to my ex-husband and that got me in trouble. I had feared doing my taxes this year with Letty onboard as an employee. But now that I had a tax boyfriend, I figured he might relish trying to do the chaos I called my taxes next year.

"I'll at least come in to keep them out of your hair." The Rockwells liked to hover and go around behind you to make sure you were cleaning to their standards. The funny thing was that our standards were actually quite a bit higher than theirs. A distraction would make Letty's job easier in the long run. As a bonus, I intended to give her all the money for it.

"Okay, just thought I'd offer," she said.

"I know and I appreciate it, but I'll take one for the team here."

She laughed, pulling the rest of her stuff out of the car. The last thing she retrieved was a little caddy stuffed with her tools that I envied fiercely. Every time I saw it I kept meaning to ask her where she got it. I missed my chance this time, too, since she was already at the door, which Mr. Rockwell opened. I'd have to remember to ask later.

I followed along behind her by about thirty seconds only to find that Mrs. Rockwell already had Letty cornered in the foyer.

"Now, I know that many people are okay with a little dust in this corner or that corner, but we here at the estate like it clean. So clean I'd like to be able to eat out of any of those corners."

I rolled my eyes before I fully cleared the front door, then went in like I owned the place.

"Fiona, how nice to see you." I took her hand and shook it, then shook her husband's. Letty, smart girl that she was, took the opportunity to scurry off in the direction of the living room.

"Oh, Tallie, I didn't realize you were going to be here. Are there problems with the help that you have to manage?"

I had been afraid she might assume that, so I shut her down immediately with my previously well-thought-out response. "Oh, gosh, no. I'm actually here to learn some tips from her. She has such a wonderful touch. I get it right, but she does it magnificently. It's hard to see her in action unless we have a house in need of a real, deep cleaning. When

I realized you were on the schedule today, I thought I'd come along." Backhanded compliment and scathing setdown all delivered in one sentence. Don't let anyone tell you that I didn't learn a thing or two during my time as one of the elite.

Fiona laughed. "It's so interesting to see you in a servile kind of position, dear. I remember when you would be the hardest party planner to please. Now, you're cleaning up after them. It must be quite a difference." And Fiona wasn't bad at the game either.

I was done playing, though. "I have a question for you while Letty does her thing. Do you guys know anything about Eli St. James? I heard you had him out here to do an assessment."

Of course, I hadn't heard anything of the kind, but Marianne had been able to access the data at the office when she went back in this morning and pulled together a few names of people I might know. Fortunately, I had three of them scheduled for today since it seemed Eli did a brisk business in the rich community.

"Are you looking to have your penthouse at the funeral home assessed?" Fiona asked with an arched, perfectly shaped eyebrow. "I hardly think your father would approve of that."

I did not roll my eyes or choke her. I would pat myself on the back later for both of those things. "Actually, I'm looking at buying a house with the money Waldo left behind, and so I started with recommendations from the man who did the assessment in the first place."

"Bad idea. Very bad idea," Mr. Rockwell—or Roll,

for short—said. Yes, he totally had people call him Roll. To go with the Rock. Don't ask.

"Why?"

The frown on his face was fierce, and the way he clenched his hand did not give me the warm fuzzies, either.

"The man was a swindler and a cheat. Any report or findings from him should not be trusted."

I kept to myself that those usually were the same thing. Another point in my favor. "Oh?" Generally, if you were vague with Roll he was happy to fill in all the blanks.

"He wanted money from us to make our house pass the assessment. Said there were too many code violations for him to be able to give us the certificate unless we could see our way to cover his expenses."

"Expenses?" Interesting.

"Yes, apparently he felt that if he was going to be able to sign the certificate, we were going to have to pay him to approve shoddy work. But my brother was the architect for the add-on, and my cousin was the builder. Both have stalwart reputations. Never did anything shoddy in their lives. Once we told him we weren't going to pay him, he started to get nasty until I threw him out on his ear."

"And you were magnificent, dear." Fiona said, petting his arm.

He puffed out his meager chest. "Of course I was. I don't need a home inspector trying to shame me into paying for something I already have. I'm smarter than that."

"Smart enough to marry me, dearest." Fiona giggled.

I almost gagged. That was three points for good behavior, and I thought I was pretty much done for the day. "So, when you didn't pay him did he threaten you?"

Roll barked out a short laugh. "He knew better. I was more than willing to let him go and try his hand elsewhere. What other people do is none of our business. But I wasn't paying him a dime more. I hired someone new immediately. We did file a formal complaint, but it didn't go anywhere. For two reasons. One, his brother is on the assessment board for the county, and two, I believe it was buried deep. How else is it that no charges have ever surfaced against him? I know plenty of people who were unhappy with his services and yet it's all been kept hushed."

So, Eli had been playing pay-me-off with the local rich people, and maybe even ones who were not so rich. And how many might have paid knowing he could lower their house's assessment so they wouldn't have to pay as much in taxes every year? Or he could jack it up and get more taxes for his brother. It was a nice little scheme. But had it gotten him killed?

I would have to look into both possibilities, though I wondered if Burton knew about this at all. And now that Eli had done something illegal, would Burton have to bring Hammond in again?

Questions to ponder later. Fiona and Roll were both talking about the pool party they were planning in six months and asked me if I knew anyone who cleaned pools, since their own pool boy had been put in jail courtesy of me several months ago. They never asked me to actually come to the party, which was fine with me. I tried to keep them entertained so Letty could do her job.

It didn't kill me, but it was close. At one point, I did step away to the powder room. Pulling out my little notebook, I sat on the closed toilet lid and made notes.

At least now I had something concrete to give Burton. I'd have preferred a killer. Yeah, never thought I'd ever say that even eighteen months ago.

Ah, how life changes.

Chapter Nine

When we finally left, I was relieved. And I was pretty sure that Letty took extra long, knowing the torture I was going through. It might have been the way she giggled as we left. Or maybe when she reminded me I used to be one of them. Possibly it was both, the brat. Once we got into our cars, I jetted to the Bean to see if Gina had heard anything or had any prophetic Scooby-Doo dreams.

Mama Shirley manned the counter and Gina was nowhere in sight. I ordered, then let Mama do her thing before I started grilling her on local gossip. Gina and I hadn't talked about whether she was going to tell her mother she was helping me so I did not want to be the one to tell her first.

"Is Gina on a break or something?" I asked nonchalantly as I sipped on a chocolate milkshake. A deviation from my normal caffeine high, but without working as hard as I normally did, I couldn't have all that excess energy racing through my veins with nothing to do and no way to get rid of it. My wrist still hurt and so did my hip. I couldn't even go to the gym or run it off. Not that I normally went to the gym, but the thought did cross my mind.

"Not a break." Mama Shirley wiped down the counter, shooting me a look that I couldn't read. I was baffled. I prided myself on being able to read them all.

"Okay." I drew the word out, not sure what else to say.

She shook her head at me. "Your Jeremy is here. My girl's trying to explain to him that her time will be taken up for a little while." Mama patted her frosted blond hair and pursed her heavily painted mouth as an angry scream erupted from the back. Not three seconds later, Gina busted through the double swinging doors like a bull through a red cape.

"He's your brother, you talk to him," she demanded.

Oh no. That was certainly not going to happen.

Jeremy came flying out behind her, his tie askew, which was so unlike him, and his normally perfectly plastered hair standing up straight. "She's your best friend, you talk to her."

Yeah, that wasn't happening, either. I looked at Mama Shirley to help me. The cagey woman just smiled and crossed her arms.

Gina whipped around and said, "You do not tell me what to do." Fortunately, the Bean was empty for once. I wouldn't be surprised if that was the only reason Mama Shirley wasn't berating her daughter for her unprofessionalism.

Groaning, Jeremy put his hands on his slim hips. "I'm not telling you anything. I asked you very nicely, at first, to please not put yourself in danger, or to follow around behind my ridiculous sister. I thought you were smarter than that."

Okay, now those were fighting words. I caught Mama Shirley's smile growing wider. I didn't care.

"Jeremy, you're a jerk." I had no problem whatsoever stepping in now.

"What?" He turned to me, his tie flapping over his shoulder. "It's true. You are ridiculous. You need a hobby, or to step up and finally take your place at the funeral home. Though I don't quite get why Dad thinks it would be a good idea to have someone who chases the dead around the actual dead."

"You bastard." I rose from my chair, taking a loud slurp of the milkshake to keep myself from saying more.

"Now you know that's not true. We both have the same mother and father, darling sister."

"Unless they found you under a rock like you used to tell me."

He snorted, the jerk. "Oh, don't start bringing up stuff like that."

"You used to tell your sister she was found under a rock?" Mama Shirley thwapped the dish towel she'd been holding over her shoulder, staring him down from across the counter.

His face flamed as he cleared his throat and smoothed his hair and then his tie. "I was young and stupid."

"And now you're older and stupider," Gina cut in.

He turned back to her in a flash. "You think I'm stupid? I don't know why you'd want to be with someone like that. Go find your dead people with my sister.

If you figure out where this all went wrong, give me a call."

That was not going to fly well with either Mama Shirley or Gina.

"You can leave," they both said at the same time with the same flat tone.

I almost felt sorry for Jeremy when he realized the gravity of what he'd said and to whom he'd said it. Almost. Until he frowned at me.

"You'd better be there tonight and be ready to explain yourself at dinner. Dad is not going to like that you went against his wishes and are looking into this. Especially when no one thinks it's a murder in the first place except you."

I did not tell him about anything I'd found out or the call from Burton. I was only going to share that with Gina. And then I wanted to get Marianne on the phone and ask her for a few files from the office.

At the moment, I would not engage him further. For both our sakes. I just kept my eyes on my brother until he gave a disgusted groan and walked out the door.

He never looked back.

Well, not until he crossed the street. His shoulders drooped and his head hung low as he looked back through the window of the Bean and zeroed in on Gina. I could have done something here, probably, but honestly, I'd promised myself when they'd first started dating a few months ago that I wasn't going to get between them. My best friend and my brother, there was no way one could win out over the other.

"I have something to get your mind off the dolt." I

sat back down and swung side to side on the stool at the lunch counter.

Gina swiped a quick fingertip under her eye. Oh no.

"He's not a dolt," she said as she sniffed. "I probably shouldn't have kicked him out. He does have concerns. Valid ones. I should have handled that better." She sat down next to me and cradled her forehead in her hands.

"Oh, honey, haven't I taught you anything?" Mama Shirley patted Gina's shoulder while laughing softly. "You let them know that you won't be bossed around from the beginning and you won't have to fight about it down the line. It's fine for him to look a little droopy walking away as long as he's coming back. I know it."

"But what if he doesn't?" Gina asked her mom in a wavering voice.

"Oh, he will," she answered. "I guarantee it. I'm sure he'll even have flowers when he does."

I envisioned Mama Shirley calling my father, who would then tell my brother that he better buy a big bouquet and come with a sincere apology. I didn't know if my dad would get involved, but he might since he wanted grandchildren as much as my mother did. In their defense, my other brother didn't even have a girlfriend who could give them grandchildren, and I had no intention of starting a family anytime soon. Jeremy and Gina, on the other hand, could be married and popping out babies within a year. Of course, my mother had already talked about it and had names picked out for the children to call her and my father. She even had a book of nursery themes for Gina to choose a décor from, too, and my mother was ready to buy it all and set it up for them. I hadn't said anything to Gina yet. I'd save that for another time.

"He's not that stupid, and he knows he crossed a line," I chimed in. "That's why he went after me next. Don't worry about it. I'm sure he'll be back with a good apology and those flowers. Maybe even some chocolates." I'd suggest it when I saw him at dinner later and told on him for fighting with Gina. That ought to make for lively conversation. It would also keep my parents from drilling me too hard for an answer about joining the funeral parlor as a partner instead of a girl Friday.

Mama Shirley winked at me, and I smiled back. We had this covered.

"So, you said you had some news to take my mind off this?" Gina also swung left to right on her stool as I did. We probably looked as if we were trying to do a synchronized stool dance.

Mama just continued to smile. "I love seeing the two of you back together. We haven't even had a snafu like that last one."

Yeah, she was talking about the one she always seemed to bring up whenever she was displeased. That one time, long ago, when I was eleven and got into trouble with Gina. She never went into details, and quite honestly I couldn't remember the circumstances, so I usually just sat through the lecture, grateful and fortunate that she didn't ever bring up the extent to which I had let Gina down when I was Mrs. Walden Phillips III and thought I was better than everyone. Maybe Gina hadn't told her much about it. I doubted that. It was more likely that Gina's mom had decided not to rock the boat we were very firmly sharing now.

"I am happy to be here. Can I have a cookie?" Why not take the advantage while I had it?

She flicked the towel at me but still put a triple chocolate chunky cookie on a plate, popped it into the microwave, then served it to me when it was warmed. Heaven, absolute heaven. Not a snickerdoodle, obviously, but definitely on par with one.

After savoring the first bite, I licked the melty chocolate off my fingers. Mama handed me a napkin. I laughed. "Yeah, I don't need that." Rolling the taste around in my mouth for another moment, I took a breath and prepared to dive in. "Now where was I? Oh, right. So, I was at the Rockwells' today, keeping them busy while Letty cleaned."

Mama groaned, and I giggled.

"Anyway, while I was there I got them talking, and it turns out they could confirm that the dastardly Eli tried to get people to bribe him to give favorable home inspections, even if the house truly was in good repair. He would try to make up things that weren't true, things people didn't know about, that could have been wrong. He banked on the hope that they wouldn't understand it and pay him to leave that off the report. He also got paid to lower the assessment so they would pay less taxes. My info is that he was working with his brother in the borough's assessment office. They'd raise the taxes for those who didn't know better and couldn't afford the bribe."

Gina leaned in, her black hair swinging forward as she put her elbows on the counter. "And no one has turned him in?"

"From what I understand the Rockwells tried to, but their paperwork got buried in bureaucracy, and once someone else did their assessment, they let it go. Maybe we should check out Eli's brother and the other guy who does inspections. The brother might not say anything depending on if he's the top dog or the underling. The other inspector guy, Mick, though, I'm thinking he has to know some dirt since he'd have run in the same circles as Eli when Eli was a home inspector instead of a code enforcer."

"Do you think the brother would have killed him? Maybe he got too mouthy or greedy?" asked Mama Shirley. Even though I missed Max intensely, I was so thankful I had these two as my backup.

"I don't know, but I think we should start by asking Marianne a few questions. She has to know something more than she's saying. Don't you think?"

The door dinged to let us know a customer was entering the store. Gina and I both turned simultaneously to find Annie walking up to the counter.

"Annie, how are you?" Mama asked first. "How's Rhoda doing with getting the place ready for this weekend?"

Annie nodded at all three of us, her light hair falling in waves over her shoulders. When she was in period costume, like a Victorian gown or a homespun dress to mimic the early colonists, she pulled it back in any number of artful ways. While wandering around town she tended to be more casual. Today she had sweats and a hoodie on. "She's making it through. Now that they've officially ruled it a heart attack without any kind of foul play, she's much better."

I bit my tongue. I needed to hear more about what

was being said in town. Blurting out my take on the situation would only make her go on the defensive and get into another passive-aggressive fight with me.

"So, she's ready to open on Friday?" Mama asked, her hand curled around her towel.

Thankfully, she, too, was playing along. Now, if only Gina wouldn't say anything to set Annie off.

A smile crossed Annie's face that lit up the room. "Oh, yes, and I can't wait to get back to work. Thanks for letting go of that crazy idea that it was a murder, Tallie."

Yeah, I still didn't say anything.

She continued as if she had the right of it. "They've been trying so hard to make sure that Paul and I had things to do around the place to earn our keep. I don't mind mowing the lawn and cleaning out the barn, but I much prefer to use my acting talents. We have a tour set up this weekend for three couples who are staying with us. It's going to be amazing. Without any issues." When she glanced my way, the smile faded. Her eyes narrowed for a second, but then she did the full-fledged smile again.

"Sounds great." If Annie caught the flat, sarcastic tone of Gina's voice, she gave no indication.

"It is. She's excited and that makes me excited for her. She deserves it and so much more for putting up with all that damage and the heartache over the years. She's like a mother to me. I love that she says the same thing to me. She never had kids, but she says she has me and Paul." She laughed softly. "And now that Paul and I can't have kids, I guess I might want to look for a stand-in kid of my own. Tallie, do you need another mom?"

"Uh . . ."

"I'm just kidding. Your mom is a gem. Now back to the reopening! In anticipation of that, I'm here to put in an order for your delicious sticky buns."

Mama Shirley got out the order pad and took Annie aside. Gina pulled me to the back room. "She seems convinced."

"I told you that no one seems to believe except you, me, and Burton. Maybe Matt, too, but that's it. We're fighting an uphill battle here."

"Let's go gird our loins then," Mama Shirley said, entering the back room.

So apparently now we were a team of four—me, Gina, Mama Shirley, and Burton. There were worse people to be in league with.

I crossed the street to my own apartment and headed upstairs without incident while talking to my uncle about the possibility of helping Marianne out with the back rent. He was willing to hold it for a short time, long enough to find out what happened and then she could make payments. He'd offered to even lower the rent, bless his heart, but I told him to hold off. He deserved payment. After all these years, he owned them outright, but he did have expenses and shouldn't lose money on them. No one seemed to be in the building and that was fine with me. I had things to do and more people to call once I hung up with my uncle.

He grudgingly agreed as I opened the door to my apartment and waited to see if Mr. Flcefers might deem me worthy of a hello. No such luck.

After going online to find the phone number for Mick O'Rourke's business, the other local inspector, I called him. I had to leave a message. And then since I couldn't reach Marianne, either, I left her a message, too.

If she didn't call me immediately I'd leave another message telling her there was a problem with the rent, and I needed to hear from her as soon as possible. That ought to get her moving.

Max picked up on the first ring. A glance at the locator app for his cell put him in the hotel. He could be in a meeting, but he sounded tired.

"Hey, sweetie," I said in a soft voice.

"Tallie, hi. What's going on?"

Nothing earth-shattering and nothing that he needed to talk with me about if he was trying to nap. Getting him off the phone quickly was my best idea in a while. If I'd known he was napping I wouldn't have called in the first place. Venting could wait. "I just wanted to hear your voice and tell you good afternoon."

"Okay." He yawned.

"Sleep well."

"I'd sleep better if you'd come with me. I told you they were willing to let me bring a guest."

And I had told him I couldn't afford it. I had jobs to do. But now was not the time to remind him of that. "Okay, well, I'll see you when you get back."

"Sounds good. Love you," he said, then must have hit the off button because the line went dead. Good enough.

So now my evening stretched out before me. I was itching to do some more research, but I had nowhere to start and nothing to work with. All government offices were closed at this time of day, Letty was done cleaning the houses, and I was . . .

Due at dinner twenty minutes ago. Crap.

I rushed down the stairs, almost tripping in my haste and knocking myself out. But I was able to safely get to my car and it started on the first try. One of these days that might not be the case, as the car was getting older and needed more maintenance than I could afford at the moment, but I wasn't ready to turn the thing in. Not yet anyway.

I made it in record time to my parents' house, but I was still late, which got me the disapproving eye from my father and the helicoptering from my mother.

"Is everything okay, dear? You look out of breath. You didn't find another dead person, did you? This really is not the way we want to increase our business, you know. Daddy has enough to do without you bringing them in to him."

I hated when she called Bud Graver Daddy. I let it pass because it was never going to change. "Everything's fine. Just a few errands to run. No more dead bodies." I sat down at the seat I'd had since I was old enough to not use a high chair. My other brother, Dylan, sat to my left, and Dad sat at the end. Jeremy sat across from me, and Mom sat to my right. For as long as I could remember everyone had the same seats. It was a tradition, and we Gravers liked our traditions.

Tonight, I would have welcomed Jeremy being anywhere except directly across from me. He kept shooting daggers from his beady eyes. I was not going to be able to enjoy what smelled like shepherd's pie if he tried to kill me with his eyes.

"You want to do this here and now?" I asked when my mother ran out of the room to get dinner from the oven and my dad took a phone call. It was business whenever and wherever for him. People didn't conveniently die between eight and five Monday through Friday.

"No, I don't want to do this at all. I want you to leave my girlfriend out of your crazy schemes and just do something with yourself."

"And what would you suggest I do when I find a dead body?"

"You didn't, Tallie, not again." Dylan scooted his chair closer to mine. "Was this one gruesome? Lots of blood, or was it pretty clean? I keep thinking that I'd like to get into the cemetery part of burial, you know, keeping the grounds and the walkways groomed. But if I do anything but landscaping and not come to the family business Dad would probably kill me."

What was it with my family and the final parts of life, or even the afterlife? Did I miss that gene somewhere?

"It was not gruesome. It was just weird. They're trying to say it was a simple heart attack when I know better."

"How?" Dylan asked.

"No one has a heart attack and has their head turned around like in *The Exorcist*, then falls neatly on a bed with their body laid out as if taking a nap," I said.

"And no one except Tallie saw him like that. Go

figure." Jeremy smirked across from me. I barely kept myself from smacking him.

"Yes, well, you can smirk all you want, but I know what I saw and Gina believes me. So while you sit here being a jerk, I'm going to figure out what really happened to Eli St. James with the help of my best friend." I kicked out at him under the table, but I was too far away.

"I can't believe you're dragging my girlfriend into your stupidity."

"What stupidity is that?" my dad asked, entering the room again.

I hadn't wanted to talk about this in front of him because he'd already told me to stay out of it. I willed Jeremy to keep his mouth shut, but of course he didn't.

"Tallie is dragging Gina into this supposed mystery with a dead guy no one else thinks has been murdered."

Dad's eyes zeroed in on me, and I could feel his censure crawling across my skin like a caterpillar, and not the nice kind.

I did not defend myself, however, because I, too, was a grown-assed woman and needed no one to tell me what I could and couldn't do.

"I thought I had asked you to stay out of that." Dad's words and tone were soft. There was no mistaking the bite of steely disappointment under them, though.

"And I believe I told you that I would be looking into it because it was important."

We faced off with my brother, Dylan, between us. He was smart and ducked down as he scooted his chair out a little to avoid the direct line of confrontation.

"I heard you," Dad finally conceded.

"Then I believe that's the end of the conversation except the part where Jeremy has demanded, like a Neanderthal I might add, that Gina stay out of things, too. Then he walked out on her, essentially ending their relationship."

"Jeremy," Mom said, coming back into the dining room with the promised shepherd's pie. I loved this stuff and was going to thoroughly enjoy it while my brother got reamed out for ruining the one relationship that could have stuck. Served him right.

He pinked right up, just as I knew he would. It went well with his tie.

I whispered the comment to Dylan and we snickered.

Jeremy's growl showed that he was not nearly as amused. "I did not end the relationship, we simply went to our separate corners so that we could think about how we wanted to end this disagreement."

Mom frowned at him. "You will end this disagreement by going to her with flowers and an apology for being a jerk. My heavens, boy, didn't you learn anything from your father?"

Jeremy crossed his arms and glared at me.

I smiled. "You might want to throw some of those fancy chocolates in, too. I hear she loves the really expensive kind from the chocolatier down the street. Nougat-filled should work. In case you didn't know."

Chapter Ten

My work done with my family at the dinner table, I went back to my apartment without having to discuss my partnership in the funeral parlor. My family did good, necessary work, and they did it with honesty and compassion. They made those final moments with your loved one special and smooth, and as painless as possible. I admired them no matter how many times I rolled my eyes at all of them, but that did not mean I wanted to be a part of it.

Someday I would come up with the right way to tell them. The right way that they'd actually believe. Until I had a brilliant epiphany on how to make that happen, I'd keep putting it off until another day. For the moment I had a cat to feed.

Mr. Fleefers met me at the door. He even twined around my ankles a few times. Of course, that was all over once I opened his fancy food.

Gina called while I was making myself tea.

"So, you can expect flowers and chocolate and an elaborate apology. Don't take anything less."

"Are you serious?" she asked.

"Absolutely. I managed to shame him in front of my parents and they demanded that he make amends. I even got out of talking about the offer my dad keeps throwing on the table for me to join the funeral home full-time." I poured boiling water over my weak tea bag, wishing it was Gina's special loose-leaf tea.

"Oh, Tallie, I hope that doesn't backfire."

"Of course it won't. I know what I'm doing. I'm sure he's out buying the necessary things now and composing an apology that will knock your socks off."

She laughed, but it sounded watery.

"Seriously, Gina, if you want out, I understand. I promised myself that I wouldn't come between you and Jeremy. If you really think he's not going to apologize, then I don't want to be the reason you break up." That would not go over well with my parents at all.

"No, it's fine. My mom was right. He needs to know from the beginning that I don't give in just because he tells me to."

"That's my girl."

"So, anything new on the investigation front?"

"Sadly, no. I left messages but that's about it. We'll just have to see what shakes out. For now."

"I'm sorry I'm not more help."

"Please. You're fine. Now, go pick out your apology acceptance outfit and we'll talk more later."

"Okay." She still sounded a little watery, but I had a feeling it was going to be all right.

I decided not to ask her to come over and help with any other research. I had a feeling it would just be more rehashing what she should have done and what he could have done. I wasn't up for that.

Once I had the parameters right I was able to find a few more things, a few one-star ratings for Eli's services, but no mention about any formal complaint. That was interesting. And his brother was up for re-election this year. Maybe he and Eli fought about ending the bribes. The brother would want to make sure as many people as possible voted for him. Maybe the brother had decided the game they were playing was dangerous, and he should back off, but Eli hadn't wanted to.

Anything was possible when I didn't have anything concrete.

I had shut down the laptop when my phone rang again. It was Marianne.

"Anything?" I asked after the standard greetings were exchanged.

"Oh, yes, Tallie, I think you're going to want to listen to the messages from the office. I found Eli's voicemail password under his phone, and there are a few messages I don't know what to do with, but others that are obviously threatening."

"His office?"

"Yes, please. And get here fast. I want to be able to share these with you as soon as possible. I hope they might answer some of your questions, although maybe they'll only raise more."

I was out the door in a flash. Gina's lights shone from her upstairs living quarters when I pulled out of the parking lot, but if my brother had decided to go apologize now, I didn't want to intrude.

Within minutes I was at the office. No lights were on, and I didn't see any cars. Had she left? Was she even going to show up? Was she the one who had killed him?

I didn't believe that last one since as far as I knew she had thought he was out getting lunch, and she'd seemed genuinely shocked that he was dead. If he'd been found in the office with a pen jammed in his throat, maybe. But out at the inn when he wasn't supposed to be there, and she hadn't known where he'd gone? I just didn't believe it.

Picking up my phone, I was about to call her when the light in the front office switched on. She beckoned me through the window and then stood by the door looking right and left constantly until I was inside.

It was a tad spooky when she slammed and locked the door behind me then flipped off the lights. Resolutely, I told myself to calm the heck down. I really should have reconsidered bringing Gina, though. I didn't know if I could actually do any damage by myself, but between us I was sure we could have taken this woman down.

I would just have to rely on my instincts and that one time I took a self-defense class, if it came down to it. Which hopefully it wouldn't.

Marianne walked behind the desk while I watched for anything weird. I kept an eye on her in case she grabbed something off the desk, like a letter opener or a stapler, with which to maim me. She did none of those things, simply hit the speaker button on the phone and dialed into the answering service. The standard woman's voice told her which options to pick and then Marianne looked up with wide eyes when she hit two buttons to make the first message

DECEASED AND DESIST 129

play. She pulled a notepad to her, chewing on the end of the pencil in her hand.

What could she have heard that would be so eraser-bite-worthy? People these days knew that nothing was ever completely erased, and it could always be used as evidence.

The first beep sounded. That was followed closely by a voice roaring through the phone,

"I don't know who you think you are, but I will take you down like the pond scum you are. I want my payment back. I want my taxes lowered. You promised me when you swindled me, and now you'd better make it happen and give me my money back, or you will pay with your neck."

That was very specific. I motioned to Marianne to give me my own paper. She tried to hand me her pencil, but I shook my head. I wanted something that hadn't been in her mouth.

I grabbed a pen from the cup on the desk and began taking notes. The next two messages were more of the same, but these threatened his head and his crotch—that one was from a woman. No one left names, and I didn't recognize any of the voices. That could be a problem, but these could maybe at least make Hammond look a little closer, or, really, look at all, if we could get him to listen to them.

The fourth message started out soft. "Mr. St. James, hi, I was wondering if you'd been able to find anything out? I really need the information so I can take my husband to court. I don't like being scared. Please call me back." She didn't leave a number or a name, probably assuming that he'd recognize her. I wished I could.

The fifth message wasn't soft, but it again didn't seem to have anything to do with building permits or inspections.

"I've been waiting five days for the information. How can I contest the will if you don't get back to me? I need to know about my wife's gambling debt, or I won't be able to keep her from inheriting. I want the money for myself and whatever I lose is coming out of your fee."

Fee? For information? Were these all confirmation that Eli had a side business snooping while he inspected? I'd tried to make that fit in my mental picture of the guy, but it hadn't computed. How would that work? He couldn't target people to let him assess their homes. That usually only happened when someone wanted to sell or refinance.

The next one answered a few questions.

"Some private investigator you are. You said that you had the case nailed shut and that all the witnesses knew not to testify, and yet some guy from the hardware store came into court today and blew my whole story out of the water. I'm not paying you a dime. And I'm not recommending you to anyone. Furthermore, if you breathe a word of what you found out while you did your investigation I will hang you until you're dead. You hear me? D-E-D!"

I couldn't help but snicker, even though it was totally inappropriate. My guy had just been threatened and the only thing I could focus on was the fact that the caller must have missed Mrs. Buzzard's second-grade spelling lessons.

"That's it." Marianne shrugged her shoulders, putting her pencil down.

I tapped the tip of my pen on the scribbles in front of me. "Are there any saved messages?"

"Nope, and these are only since Eli went missing. I think it must be a different line, maybe, because I never got a call like this from anyone."

"Can you access the voicemails from your line?"

"No, I tried but I don't have access."

Okay, so we had some threats and some information but nothing to really go on. Although I did have a new avenue. If Eli had been working on the side as a private investigator, he could have crossed the wrong person who did not want a secret out. It confirmed what Mrs. Koser had been saying about Eli asking about her children.

This opened up a whole new can of worms, but maybe it would finally be one that Hammond wouldn't turn his nose up at.

"I started looking for a new job," Marianne said quietly, doodling on her notepad.

"How's it going?"

"Everyone so far has said that if I have Eli's ethics, then they have no room for me." She shook her head.

I tried to think of anyone who might need an assistant. Unfortunately, I came up dry at the moment. "Maybe you should just leave Eli off your résumé and pretend like you just got here."

"Wouldn't that be dishonest? And I know how these little towns work, everyone knows everyone's business. If they asked around they'd know that I hadn't sent in a correct application."

"There is that." I fiddled with my paper, not knowing what else to do for her.

"Maybe I should just go home. It's not better there,

but at least I know what I'm dealing with. This town is pretty messed up in a lot of ways."

I'd never thought of it like that. I guess we did have some pretty interesting characters. To someone who hadn't grown up here a lot of the townspeople could seem downright strange. To me they were the norm.

"Don't give up just yet. Go back to the last one and let them know you were not aware of anything he had going on. You could even tell them you didn't know about his side business, that he kept you in the dark. Use me as a reference." I needed her to stay around for a little bit. I couldn't have her wandering off when she was the only one with access to the office.

"Yeah, I don't know what I want to do." Pulling a corner off her paper, she shrugged.

"While you're deciding, is there a way to save these messages?" I'd thought of recording them on my phone from the speakerphone but I had a feeling Hammond would not go for that, and I didn't want to have to defend myself again. He already thought I was crazy.

"I'll try to figure something out."

"Okay, just don't erase them while you're trying."

"I'll try not to." She stuck her tongue in the corner of her lips as she hung the phone up. I didn't have a good feeling about this, but I wanted to look around while we were in here to see if maybe he had any files. Of course, I knew all about the risks of handing over information that I hadn't obtained by the right channels. I didn't care at this point, though. I'd come up with creative ways to explain how I'd gotten it before, and I'd do so again if I had to.

"Are there any filing cabinets around here that

you're not supposed to go in?" I asked, prowling the office. As far as I knew it was the front room, a small bathroom, and this office. Not an expensive operation and part of a strip mall. It was still worth asking.

"There's one in the closet over there. I think that's it. He warned me the first day that it's his personal information. Do you think he might have kept his private-eye things in there? Maybe that's where he keeps all the files on these people who are calling!" Her eyes widened and her innocence was either real or a ploy to get me to believe her so she could do more bad things.

I'd experienced both kinds of people, so I wasn't putting anything past her. She could shove me in the closet, leave, and then do nefarious things, and I wouldn't be able to stop her. But I'd keep my eyes peeled and my back guarded. I'd also made every effort to avoid being surprised.

I really wished I had brought Gina with me, dammit.

When I found the filing cabinet tucked into a closet, I tried every drawer, and they were all locked. Of course they were. And when I asked for the key, Marianne had no idea where it might be. I guess probably on his key ring if it held the paperwork I thought it might.

I was not handy with picking locks, and honestly, I had none of those fancy tools. I didn't want to damage anything just in case it was important— Burton or Hammond would have a fit if I tampered with stuff. But, boy, did I want in those drawers.

There was no hope for it, though. I was going to have to wait and see if the messages and the threats, along with the complaint that never made it past the

shred bin, were enough for Hammond to look into
Eli's murder.

I considered asking Marianne where Eli lived and
seeing if I could get in there. In the end, I decided it
wouldn't do me any good.

There were some lines drawn in hard concrete.
Breaking and entering was one of those. If I thought
my family was not happy about me looking into a
murder that no one thought had happened, I hated
to think about what their reaction would be if I actually got arrested and they had to bail me out.

"Be careful," I said on my way out to the front of
the office. Marianne followed me.

"I will. I'll be leaving soon, once I figure out how to
save the messages, then I will let you know where you
can get them. Thanks for coming over, Tallie."

"Of course, just please be safe."

"Absolutely." Marianne smiled. I still worried.

And worrying about her kept me from seeing the
cop car parked next to mine.

"I'm not going to the station," I told Matt. He hadn't
tried to reach for my wrists to cuff them, and he
hadn't made any moves to make me get in the car, or
even follow him, yet. He just asked me nicely.

"What am I supposed to do, Tallie? I just caught
you walking out of a dark office. I know for a fact you
don't have keys for that place."

"No, I don't, but I was in there at the invitation of
the secretary who has some voicemails that I think
Hammond is going to want to listen to."

"I doubt it. Hammond doesn't want anything from

you, or haven't you figured that out yet? He's a hard-ass with something to prove. Any help from you isn't even on his list. And I didn't see anyone else. Why didn't she walk out with you to lock the door behind you?"

"She was trying to figure out a way to save the voice-mails so they could be listened to later. She should be out in a minute." But then I remembered that her car must have been around back because it wasn't out here with mine. It must have been somewhere since I doubted she'd walked this far. Would she answer the door if I knocked again? Or would it still be unlocked? It was worth a try.

I pulled the door to me and it opened. "See, it's un-locked. She must still be in the office. Follow me, and maybe you can listen to the messages for yourself so you can report to Hammond that they're worth listen-ing to. That takes me at least one more step out of the equation."

I was pretty pleased with that idea until I walked into Eli's dark office. The dark office with no Mari-anne in sight. I flipped the light on at the wall switch and took in the pristine desk, the bare walls, and the phone on the desk. It looked as if no one had been there at all.

I hustled over to the back door, hoping that her car would still be there. Maybe she had saved the mes-sages and was just heading out. I didn't completely believe that, but I still wanted to check. I was pretty sure I had just been left high and dry in an office that didn't belong to me, with no one to back up my reason for being here.

Not surprisingly, there were no cars in the back lot. Change of plans then.

Running to the file cabinet, I tried to find any hint of damage or that they had been opened. I couldn't find anything except that when I pulled on the drawers this time they flew open with only a little tug. They were completely and utterly empty. Had they been empty before? How had Marianne gotten them open when I couldn't? Did she really have a key and just refused to tell me? Did she take whatever was in them? The files that I thought had to do with Eli St. James's private-eye business?

Holy crap. Matt looked at me with crossed arms as I stood in the closet with what I was sure was a horrified expression on my face.

"You want to tell me anything before I take a look in those drawers, or ask why you would be looking in them in the first place? Or how about, why you would even be here when no one else is? How did you get in?"

I frantically looked behind the cabinet and under the cabinet, then felt around the closet shelf above the cabinet, while he continued talking to me. I wanted to look out the back door again, just in case she had dropped anything on her way out. Something, anything, that would make me look better.

I had to struggle against Matt's grip on my arm to open the door and see if there were any cars in the parking lot. Still nothing.

I shook him off. "I'm not going to try to run away, you imbecile. I'm aware how bad this looks, but I swear I didn't do anything but meet Marianne here, and she let me in. I wouldn't know the first thing about picking locks and especially not that industrial one on the front door." Thank God that was true, or I would be in even deeper trouble than I could feel sucking at my knees right now.

"This doesn't look good."

I sighed and closed my eyes, turning from him so he couldn't see. "Are you going to have to call Hammond?"

"I think so."

This was not good.

Chapter Eleven

I did not particularly like the inside of our small jail at the back of the police station. It was more of a holding cell than a jail, but it still had bars that I would have rattled if only they'd given me a tin cup.

When asked if I wanted to call anyone before Hammond got there, I asked to see my cell phone for Marianne's number. No surprise that she didn't answer, but I had been hoping. That hope crashed to the floor just like the drunk guy that my cousin brought in thirty minutes later. Matt looked at me once, shook his head, and then went about his business.

I was not going to wake up Gina, or any of my family. Calling Max wouldn't help. He was across the country, and no matter how much I wanted him here he couldn't help at the moment. I'd just sit here until Hammond came in, explain my story, and hope that he would believe me this time. That hope was slim, I knew it. It was all I had at the moment, though. That and a plastic bottle of water.

"Not even coffee?" I asked the officer who'd been

watching over me while Matt had been called out for the drunk guy. I didn't know him well. Gary Steinman had started here about a year ago, bringing his family with him from Long Island, New York, in search of something more slow-paced with more of a community aspect. We had that in spades when people weren't killing each other.

"Nope, sorry, no coffee. It's against the rules, and I stay within the rules. You should have done the same thing."

Wonderful, not only a jailer but also one with a moral compass that he was going to try to shove down my throat. "Whatever happened to innocent until proven guilty?"

"I'm not the one to talk to about that, that's Hammond. I do believe he just pulled up around back."

My palms started sweating and I wished desperately for something to calm myself. Maybe I should have at least called Gina to talk me down instead of thinking I knew what I was doing and how I would do it without any kind of help. What had I gotten myself into?

I had always seen two-way mirrors in movies. They were a standard in any cop drama. Seeing them from the inside was a different experience. One I was not happy about in the least.

There was only me and Hammond in the room, so either he was both the good cop and the bad cop, or maybe just the bad without the counterpart.

I warned myself not to forget that for some reason he did not like me. Had this been Burton I might have had a better chance. We'd always bantered even as I'd pissed him off by doing whatever I wanted. And I'd done whatever I'd had to do since I had needed to get him to take me seriously several times in the last year. He'd come through grumbling, yet he was still open to my ideas when I threw them on the table.

This guy was another story. One I didn't want to hear. In other words, the man across from me was a whole different animal.

His eyes were narrowed and his jaw firmly clenched. I would get no quarter here. It would benefit me greatly to remember that. Maybe I should have made my one call to Burton. At least then I might have had a hope in hell of getting out of this unscathed.

Since the time for the decision was way past, I now needed to think about how I was going to handle Hammond.

Did I want to rail and tell him to get me out of here pronto because he knew I hadn't broken into Eli St. James's office? Yes, absolutely, but once I saw his fist clench on his pen to the point where he almost broke it, I knew it was a bad approach.

Of course I knew it before, but I had been trying to talk myself into it. The angst started the moment he'd walked in the station's back door right by my cell without making eye contact, and then made me wait an additional forty-five minutes before he came to see me. There wasn't another soul here except the drunken guy who was happily snoring away on a cot.

I opened my mouth to say hello, and he nailed me with a glare.

"Don't say a word. I let you sit in the cell for so long because I wanted to make sure I didn't come in after you and start shouting."

Okay, so bad cop with a tinge of good? With a want to be good but not quite pulling it off? I wasn't sure, but I really felt that keeping my mouth shut just this once would serve me best. I didn't even nod to acknowledge that I'd heard him.

"Nothing to say?"

I also resisted the urge to roll my eyes. Hadn't he just told me not to say a word? Now he was berating me for not talking? What the heck? But I didn't fall for it. I simply shook my head.

"Well, you must really know you're in trouble and don't want to piss me off. I'm not Burton, am I? Good thing you know that." He leaned back in his chair with some kind of folder as if he had all the time in the world. And why wouldn't he when he wasn't out chasing me around, or any of the real bad guys, for that matter?

That thought I also kept to myself.

"So, I have that the officer found your car outside the strip mall and then saw you exiting the building with no lights on. Is that correct?"

"Yes, but . . ."

"Just answer the questions with yes or no. No additional conversation."

Good God, did he know what he was asking? He absolutely did. There was no misinterpreting how he looked pissed enough to send me back into the cell without letting me say another word. There, he would let me only sing the jailhouse blues if I didn't play along.

I felt sick to my stomach, the desire to dry heave almost overwhelming me. I should have called my dad, or even Mama Shirley, and asked them to intervene for me here. Burton came to mind, again, and it took all I had not to go ahead and ask for my phone call now. I'd lay down odds that even with a pissed-off Burton, this would not have been so bad.

"Yes," I said in response to his statement about one-word answers, just in case he needed proof that I was willing to follow his directives. For now.

"And then when you went back in, you had knowledge of right where the filing cabinets were?"

"Yes." I clamped my mouth shut after the short word. That way I wouldn't expound about anything else, like Marianne being there, or how I didn't know until she told me. I was not going to sign a statement that did not have those things in it, though. He'd just have to get over himself.

"And then you tried to leave through the back door even though the officer was right behind you?'

"No." There was a ton of vehemence behind that one word. I seethed and seethed that he would think I would do something like that. If Matt had told him that, then I was going to bean him at the first opportunity.

Hammond looked up finally. I'm sure he could see that I was barely leashing myself, but he went back to his paper as if I hadn't looked ready to jump across the table.

"And you say you were there with the secretary? The one you were caught with the other day in the same office?"

"Yes and yes."

"I think that's all." He stood and turned toward the door.

I, of course, exploded out of my metal chair like a

hound of hell. "You have got to be kidding me! That's it? That's all. You just want me to sit here like a docile little doll and answer your stupid questions without also telling you that Marianne called me and invited me down. I can show you her cell phone number in my phone. She also dialed the voicemail and played a bunch of messages that were threats to Eli. She was the one who told me where the filing cabinets were. When I left they were locked and closed. I was going to call the station in the morning and see if you could get a warrant to search the premises with the new information Marianne gave me. I don't know why she didn't tell you."

He turned back around, so I drew in a breath and rammed head-on.

"I do know why she didn't tell you, because you're a jerk and don't listen to anything that doesn't go along with what you want. You're perfectly willing to feed me to the craft wolves and get me a hobby, but you don't believe me, and you probably never will. Go, Officer Hammond, go type up your report about my answers and make sure to bring me it with a red pen because I'm going to mark that thing up until you think your poor little eyes are bleeding."

He stared at me for a few seconds while I let my chest heave. "You done now?"

"Yes, let me go back to my cell and sit there. I'll call my mother in the morning and have her pick me up unless you feel the need to keep me."

"Fine."

"Not fine," Burton said from the door I had not heard open during my tirade.

Hammond and I stared at each other for one full

minute. I didn't know whether to be pleased that Burton was here or scared that now I would have two people against me, both police officers, both capable of charging me with a crime I hadn't committed. Burton had asked me to look into things, of course. That didn't mean he'd stand up for me when I was in trouble. Like now.

"Hammond, you're excused." Burton never took his eyes off me.

"Sir, you're on administrative leave and have no say here."

"This is still my station, so I do have a say. I will finish this interview. You go home. We'll talk tomorrow."

"But . . ." He trailed off when Burton focused his gaze on him. So, I wasn't the only one who faltered under that laser-sharp, silent reprimand.

"I'll go, but this is my case. I will not have anyone mess it up."

Those sounded like fighting words to me. And to Burton, too, if his narrowed eyes and pulsing vein in his neck were any indication.

Even I wouldn't have gone that far. That was saying something.

Burton and I both waited for Hammond to get up from the table and make his way out the door. Burton held out his hand for the folder, and the hesitation from Hammond caused a tension that could have been cut like a hot knife through ice cold butter. Finally, he handed it over and left with a grunt. Burton placed a call to the front desk, then waited until he had confirmation that Hammond had left before sitting down across from me.

"You know what, Tallie, you are one of the most

frustrating and complex people I've ever had the pleasure to meet and watch grow up." He perused the paperwork in front of him that I so desperately wanted to see.

"I wasn't doing what that report says I was doing."

"Let's wait and see what is here." He kept reading, his lips moving but no sounds coming out.

The suspense was killing me. Was he going to drill me with the same questions? Not let me answer as Hammond had done? Why wouldn't he just say something? Anything!

Chapter Twelve

After what felt like an eternity but was really probably only two minutes, Burton looked up. "I'm surprised at your short answers. I always seemed to have to listen to you ramble. Here you only go with yes or no."

I straightened in my chair, folding my hands on the scarred table. "I was very specifically told to only give yes or no, and he looked like he might gladly have me shot at dawn if I didn't comply."

He scoffed. "Come on now, Tallie. Hammond can be tough, but he wouldn't have had you shot at dawn."

"That's not what his body language was saying."

Tilting his head to the left, he studied me. "So, if my body language was harsher do you think you'd listen to me, too?"

"Nope," I said, finally feeling at least a little bit safer with the knowledge that, though Burton and I might not always see eye to eye, he usually came around to my way of thinking. Eventually.

"So, tell me what happened." Sitting back, he seemed to settle in for a long story.

I wasn't sure why I had to do this, since he was the one who had asked me to look into it. But if it was for the record, to go against my one-word answers to Hammond, then I was willing to play along. I gave him the rundown from the beginning, all the way back to falling off the ladder after finding Eli St. James dead and staring sightlessly from the bed. Burton grunted, blew out his breath a few times, and once made a disgusted noise, but he mostly stayed silent as he let me get the whole story out. I was impressed and grateful, but also still baffled why he was acting like this was all new to him when he knew what had happened.

Or I was baffled until he responded. Then I was befuddled.

"That's a pretty impressive tale and a little hard to believe."

And my balloon was popped. Of course it was. Why had I truly thought he was going to give me permission to look into this, effectively begging me to be his eyes on the ground? It wasn't the first time he'd turned tail on me. "And yet that's how it happened." I waited for his response. I'd been doing a good job for the most part and I wanted to continue to help, but he had to believe me first.

"What are you doing?" I asked.

He shook his head at me.

"Seriously, I have to know."

Again with the headshaking. This time he also added some hand gestures. With his hand resting on the wooden table, he curled his fingers and thrust his palm out at me as if he was aiming to break my nose. I scooted back in my chair. Next, he made a fist, then crossed his fingers before giving me a thumbs-up. What the heck?

He wanted to break my nose, punch me, go back on his promise, but I was doing a good job?

"Can I go now?" I had a headache and was done playing games.

"I'll walk you out." He tugged at his ear, then put his finger next to his right eye.

Tallie, out.

"I don't think that's necessary. I can find my way out."

And if he was under the impression I wasn't going to take him to task for messing with me, he was sadly mistaken. It wouldn't be now, where he could easily throw me back into the slammer, but it would be soon. And I knew it would be brutal.

Looking into these things by myself when I had something at stake was one thing, but doing them when Burton asked and then being put on the headsman's block and threatened with hand gestures was not something I appreciated. In the least. Wretched, wretched man!

He obviously did not take my not-so-subtle hint that I wanted away from him and fast when he rose as I did. He held the door for me. It took all I had to stay the urge to bring on the violence. I almost kicked him in the shins, just because I could. But the cells were right outside the door, so I put one foot in front of another instead of up his lying, manipulating rear end.

We passed Suzy, who gave me a sad smile, and Matt, who looked like he was going to say something before he clamped his mouth shut. Fine, give me the walk of shame when I'd done nothing wrong. I had been freaking *asked* to look into things. By the very man who was following me on my walk of shame, dammit!

Burton and I made it out the front door. I was about to take off at a run when Burton rested his hand on my arm.

I tried to shake him off, but he held on. Chalk up one more deduction of points for my least favorite person at the moment. At least Hammond was direct about being a jerk. Burton had snowed me quietly, and I was not taking it well.

"I'm not doubting you," Burton said. I snorted but he rolled right over the sound. "Come on, Tallie. I was getting the facts so I could have Matt call this Marianne and find out her side of the story. I couldn't say I wasn't pissed about what you're doing, even though I know you've been asked to stop it. I have to maintain neutrality, but you always have good information, no matter how you get it. I have to keep Hammond off-balance or he'll tromp all over everything."

"What was with the gestures? The punching hands?" I unbent long enough to ask.

"Girl, I know you took sign language in third grade. I taught it to you myself. I was trying to tell you there are eyes and ears in the room. I can't appear to be asking you to do this."

Was I supposed to say thank you after sitting in that tiny room, not knowing if I was going to be released or not? I wouldn't do it.

"I'm not going to be able to help much with this one, Tallie." Burton looked back at the building with his arms crossed. "Hammond was right that I'm out on leave and have little authority until I get back. I don't know what he's doing, but I have a couple of people watching him just in case. He's not without his skeletons in the closet, if you know what I mean."

And now I had another person to look up on the internet. Or I could ask Matt once I got over being mad at him for arresting me and putting me in a freaking jail cell. My mom and his mom were going to be talking about that for days.

"And what am I supposed to do?" I asked, still wondering what was going on here. "I can't just sit back and hope that Hammond gets a clue. Someone murdered that man. Rhoda now has a murder scene that she cleaned and has a person due to stay in the room in a few days. All evidence is ruined because of your replacement. Someone left that room as I fell off the ladder. Hammond doesn't want to know that. He's walking a very thin line on some pretty shady stuff. There has to be a story there. The bad guy who did this needs to be caught. What if they think I saw him and come after me next?"

"I did think of that, contrary to what you believe about me. And so I'm going to make you a deal."

A deal? This was new. What would it entail? I was almost afraid to ask, but it almost sounded like Burton really was on my side. Wouldn't that be a nice change?

"I'm going to let you go. If you could, in some way, get ahold of this Marianne, then we could bring her in and ask her to verify why she left and if she actually did leave with the files you think were in the cabinet. That way we get you off altogether. It's standard protocol to put anyone suspected of committing a crime into the cell for their protection and for ours. I can't bend the rules. I'm not bending them now when I let you walk out under your own steam. You don't have to call your mom or anyone else unless you want to. Up to you." He took a step back. He turned to walk back into the station, then turned back around. "Let me know when you get in touch with Marianne. We'll go pick her up. And you might want to take Gina with you from now on, just to make sure you have someone else who went through the whole thing with you and can vouch for you."

Okay, I'd said my balloon was popped before, but now I felt like the balloon that had burst and then got caught on the bottom of someone's shoe with dirty bubble gum. Yeah, not the best feeling. I was being given freedom but being chastised for not doing the smart thing at the same time.

Although, there was one thing I did need to clarify before he walked away. "So, you believe me?"

"I can't confirm or deny that until we speak with Marianne. Let's just say that if I truly believed you had broken into Eli's office, you'd be back behind the bars instead of wandering around out on the streets. Keep in touch. I won't be able to help much, but if you share your information with me, maybe we can see why Hammond is so bent on destroying you. And why he refuses to look at this as anything more than a natural death." With that he turned around again and left me standing in the parking lot.

To say that Gina was not pleased with my decisions the night before would have been a gross understatement. She'd yelled, cursed, and then finally asked for all the details. I gave them to her and she

shook her head over scones and regular coffee. None
of that fluffy seven-name stuff for me this morning. I
had things to do and people I needed to do them.

"If you're done I think we need a battle plan."

"Of course we do. Let me get a sticky bun." She set
down a plate between us at the front counter. There
were a few people in the shop, but this was a downtime and most of the ones here were hard of hearing.
Besides, at this point, I didn't care who heard. Maybe
more people would keep their eyes out for Eli's murderer and now Marianne, who I had not been able to
get ahold of.

I took a napkin from the dispenser and a pencil
and began making a list. "We need to find Marianne,
and I'd like Matt to look into the other contractor. I'm
going to ask Uncle Sherman to get a feel for Eli's
brother. As the city's fire chief, he knows the players.
I don't want to give that to Burton, or Hammond,
without first making sure my story sticks. I'm done
with being doubted."

"It happens to all of us, Tallie, you more than others
because of your history."

My history of cutting everyone who had mattered
to me out of my life after I'd married and thought I
was better than everyone else. It didn't pass my notice
that most people had forgiven me without much fuss.
I should be thankful for that, but sometimes I wished I
had never married Waldo at all so that I wasn't in this
position. Then again, being in this position also had
to do with me getting too involved in things that
weren't my business. I wasn't going to admit that right
now, though. I wasn't even going to think about it.

This was my business as of last night. If I had to go to jail for something I didn't do, then by God I was going to get that justice and ram it down someone's throat.

"Okay, so history aside. We need to find Marianne first. I don't have anything that Letty needs help with this afternoon, and no other obligations the rest of the day, so I'm going to make some headway on this."

Gina nodded. "Understandable. And what do I do since you cut me out of things last night?"

"That wasn't intentional."

"And yet you still did it." She buffed a spot on the lunch counter, not looking at me. "Your brother did come over to apologize with flowers, chocolates, and a card. He said he'd put a piece of jewelry on order for me, but I don't want to think about that until it's in my hand."

"Do you want it to be a ring?" They'd been dating for only a few months, but they'd known each other for years and had almost gotten together before. I would love Gina as a sister-in-law, more than anyone else. But I didn't know if it was too soon.

She took a napkin out of the dispenser and twirled it around on the countertop with her index finger. "I don't know." She looked up with a wrinkled forehead. "Is that bad?"

Grabbing her hand, I squeezed her fingers. "Absolutely not. And even if it is a ring, you don't have to answer right away."

"If it's a ring, she'd better say yes before he even finishes asking the question," Mama Shirley said behind me.

I hadn't known she was there, she could be stealthy

like that. Gina hadn't known either from the way her ears flamed.

"Mom, we've talked about this before and it's all up in the air. We have years. It doesn't have to be right now. I want to make sure we're on the same page about things before I even consider something like marriage. I want it to be forever, and forever doesn't have to start this second."

So different from the way I had wanted Waldo to get me out of my situation when I'd said yes to his proposal.

"Fine, fine, but know what your heart wants and then go for it. Don't wait too long."

"I won't, but right now Tallie and I are working on finding that woman Marianne."

"Red hair, big glasses, new to town?" Mama Shirley leaned a hip against the counter.

Of course Mama would know all about her. "Yes."

"She usually comes by the front of the shop and looks longingly at the cakes before she power walks up Arch Street."

How did she get here? Did she drive and park her car, then get back in her car to go to work? There was no way she walked here from her rental then walked to work. "Every day? At the same time?"

"Pretty much. She was late one day, but I saw her stop at the bank so that could have been why. She works for that man you girls are looking into, doesn't she? Why do you think she's missing?"

I let Gina give her mom the rundown on what happened last night and then endured the swat I got on the arm for not taking Gina with me, or at least letting her know where I was going in case something had happened.

"I won't do it again."

"See that you don't. You girls are a pair. Even if this went weird for a little while, you're more a pair now than you ever were. You're not alone anymore, Tallie, you remember that."

"I will." I gulped to hold back the tears threatening my eyes at that one phrase. *Not alone anymore.* And I wasn't.

The door opened and closed. Mama's eyes narrowed and I wondered who it might be. When I turned, I found myself looking at a not-very-happy Annie.

"Why are you still looking into this?" she demanded. "I told you what the police found and that should be good enough for you. Rhoda is a good woman and doesn't deserve to be treated this way."

I rocked back in my chair. What was she talking about?

"Now, Annie, calm down." Mama pulled a to-go cup from the rack and filled it with a fragrant roast.

"I can't," the other woman said. "Rhoda is at the house crying because Tallie is looking into this as a murder and it's going to make people cancel their plans for this weekend. It's supposed to be the grand opening and she's already lost two reservations."

"She has?"

Annie turned to me at my words. "Yes, she has. She's beside herself. A murder on the property certainly isn't something you want to put up on the website, but the gossip has gotten around. Two of the people were out-of-towners related to people who live here. They heard about the murder from their relatives and have decided to stay at that new cheap chain hotel on the freeway instead of Rhoda's bed-and-breakfast."

God, I hadn't expected that. I assumed, since I was one of the few who actually thought it was murder, that no guests would give any credence to the rumor.

But even lost reservations for my family friend didn't stop me from wanting to know who did this.

"I'm sorry." It wouldn't do much, but I truly was sorry.

"Then you should stop looking because you might not like what you find at the end of your trail."

"Now, what does that mean?" Gina asked, beating me to the punch.

Annie's gaze dropped to the floor. When she lifted her eyelashes, they were wet with tears. "I'm just saying that I know there wasn't anyone else there on Monday. I didn't do it, Paul didn't do it, Arthur didn't do it. I think it would be better if you left things alone, Tallie. From what I understand, he wasn't a good guy and the world is better without him." She accepted the cup from Mama, handing over a five-dollar bill.

Mama pushed it back with a shake of her head. "On the house."

"Thank you." She turned back to me. "I don't know what happened, but if the coroner is willing to go with heart attack and the police think the same thing, then maybe this time you should just let it go."

With that she left the Bean.

Mama, Gina, and I exchanged glances.

I was the first one to speak. "I'm sorry, but even if it's Rhoda, I don't think I can let it go. There's a part of me that wants to just walk away and not ruin the woman's life, but I can't. I'm in too far to back out, and whoever did it has no right to take a life, no matter how much of a jerk Eli was." I rose from my chair. "Besides, I know that there were other people there. Two cars pulled in while I was cleaning the windows out front. Whoever they were, it's possible that one of them is the killer. We have to find Marianne and look further into these files. I need to know who Eli had information on so we can start narrowing this down."

"She still hasn't come by and that's unusual," Mama said. "I wonder where she could be. You should go out and check her house again. Gina, you go with her. I've got the counter for a little while. Everything's done in the oven for the next hour until lunch. Go, see what you can find."

If Mama was giving permission, then I was not going to be the one to turn her down.

I felt a lot like Thelma and Louise off on a jaunt of illegal proportions when we first went to the office and found nothing. Next, we went to Marianne's house. I heard Peanut barking up a storm and didn't want to set her off more than she already was.

It couldn't be helped, though. We walked up the porch steps and tiptoed around ceramic sunflowers and frogs to get to the front door. I knocked and Gina and I stared at each other as Peanut went nuts, barking and pawing at the front door.

She started bouncing against the door, and I was afraid a neighbor might call the cops. I certainly didn't need Hammond coming out here to answer a call about me. Again.

I was about to walk away and just call Marianne

again when the door creaked and then flew open under the pressure of the huge dog. Peanut scrambled out of the house with her mouth open wide and I could have sworn I was a goner to the jaws of death named Peanut.

Chapter Thirteen

Gina cowered behind me as I braced myself to be eaten by a huge Saint Bernard. Squinching my eyes shut, I waited for the first bite, hoping the dog was up-to-date with her rabies vaccination. Not that it would help me if she killed me with her jaws, but at least I wouldn't have rabies on top of everything else.

But nothing happened. Whining reached my ears just as I felt a gentle tug on the bottom of my T-shirt. I peeked out under my lashes to find Peanut sitting on her rear end with the tail of my shirt in her jaws, pulling in small increments.

"I think she wants us to follow her. Look at her eyes, they're so sad." Gina shoved me forward, surprising me into taking a step over the threshold.

Peanut let go immediately to run into the house. When she realized we weren't following, she came back and sat in the doorway whining.

"Okay, girl." Gina moved into the house. I was the one tugging on a shirt this time, trying to keep Gina from going into someone else's house without permission and possibly walking into something we were not equipped to deal with. Why else would Peanut be whining and Marianne not coming to the door?

But once Gina was ten feet away from me, I couldn't stay behind.

I wound my way through the bulky furniture in the tiny house, taking in everything I could lay my eyes on. Nothing appeared disturbed, or at least not that I could tell since there was so much of it. But nothing was overturned and everything was crammed posterior-to-elbow in the house, so I was relatively sure it would be obvious if something was messed up.

Peanut went to the back of the small house and sat in the bedroom doorway. I really didn't want to go in, but Gina was already in there, talking in low tones.

When I rounded the corner I saw Marianne spread out over the bed, blood dribbling out of her mouth and her hair all over the place—more than all over the place since it was actually lying two feet from her. A wig? Why was she wearing a wig when she had a full head of platinum-blond hair?

That was a question for later, though, because I had to do something I absolutely wanted to avoid.

I had to call Hammond.

"Don't touch anything," I told Gina as I dialed the very familiar number.

"She's breathing, but I don't know how bad it is," Gina reported. "She's not responding to anything I say. She's totally knocked out.

"Hello, Tallie," Suzy answered. "What happened now?"

"Suzy, this is serious. I'm at Marianne's house. Hammond, or someone else—just someone—needs to come out here now. Marianne is unconscious and bleeding. She's Eli St. James's secretary and might be targeted because of his death."

"Oh, dear Jesus. I'm sending someone out right now."

Within minutes we had an ambulance on the small street. Gina stayed with Marianne while I went out front to direct the ambulance. A few neighbors tried to ask me what had happened, but I didn't have answers so I ignored them. My mind was racing with the possibilities and the questions and the non-answers in all of this.

I was so tempted to look for the files before Hammond got here, but I didn't want to touch anything. It didn't stop me from looking around while the EMS professionals did their thing. I kept my hands behind my back to make a visual scan, nothing more.

A police officer showed up just as I spotted the edges of several folders sticking out of a magazine rack crammed with issues of *Better Homes and Gardens* from the eighties. With great restraint I did not touch it. Instead, I stood guard at the front of the house so I could make sure no one else was coming in and out. I was tired of people disappearing when I needed them to be where they said they were going to be. I was also tired of feeling like an idiot, expecting people to not lie to me.

Who was Marianne? Was that even her name? I had trusted way too easily again. Had she killed Eli and then pretended to know nothing about it to get her hands on the files? To do what with them? Maybe she knew all about the filing cabinet and was in on the private-eye thing. Maybe she was the one who was actually running it since Eli seemed to need a handler for other things. So many questions and not an answer in sight.

I waved the officer on through to the bedroom while continuing to stand at the magazine rack, not moving. I wasn't certain these were the right files. They could be coupons or articles she'd cut out. For all I knew, they could be pictures of Peanut.

I wasn't going to touch a thing. I promised myself, and I tried hard to keep my promises to myself if no one else.

They wheeled Marianne out with Gina following close behind.

"I hope she's going to be okay," Gina said, softly. "They couldn't tell immediately if anything was broken. The blood in her mouth looks like someone punched her hard enough to knock her unconscious, and they think maybe that person ran when Peanut came after him. The poor dog doesn't know what to do with herself without Marianne here."

"If that's her real name," I said as I spotted Matt pulling up at the curb.

"Yeah, I saw the wig, too. What do you think it means?" Gina asked. "Do you think she was hiding out? I wonder if she was working with Eli instead of for him."

I leaned on the wall, still not touching anything else. "I wonder a lot of things, but that is definitely on the top of the list. I think I found the folders containing Eli's private-eye info. I promised myself I wouldn't touch them."

"Thank God for small miracles," Matt said.

I wasn't sure if he was talking about me finding

the folders, or not touching them. I wasn't going to ask that either, I was just happy he was here so Hammond didn't immediately take me in for whatever he could come up with. I pointed at the magazine rack and stepped back.

He used gloves to pick them out of the magazines and then moved toward the front door. It didn't look like there was a whole filing cabinet there, but I had no idea how many there might be. I told Matt as much when he asked.

"She never gave any indication that she was wearing the wig?"

"No, to that, too. I had no idea her hair wasn't her own."

"Well, we're going to look into some things and definitely take Eli's death more seriously now."

At least there was that. I didn't say it, but I was definitely thinking it.

"I'm sorry we didn't take you more seriously, but you have to understand that without any evidence I wasn't able to move forward." Matt ran a hand over his chin.

I just looked at him because there was no answer I could give him that wouldn't sound rude. And I was still pissed that he'd thrown me in jail last night. My mom didn't know, yet. If she found out, there would be a serious penalty to pay for both of us.

"Okay then." He sighed and took out his phone. "I'm going to have to call the pound. We don't know how long the victim will take to recover from her injuries. I can't leave the dog here the whole time. Not to mention that we need to be able to search the house from top to bottom for evidence without having a hundred pounds of fur following us around and getting in the way."

Gina turned pleading eyes on me, and I shook my head. I knew what she was asking. I wasn't going to do it. No way. No how.

"Please," she mouthed. "I can't."

"Yes, you could," I whispered back.

"No, I really can't. Because I make so much of my food upstairs or use it as a test kitchen, I signed an agreement that I wouldn't have anything furry living in my apartment, or the building."

"But I can't either. Not only would my dad freak, but Mr. Fleefers would have a major meltdown. I don't want to do that to him."

"Look at her, though." Gina pointed at the poor puppy who had sat on her rump again. This time she wasn't whining so much as she was crying. Peanut kept looking at the front door and then back toward the bedroom, then back at the front door. She hung her head with her mouth turned down. Oh God, she was pulling at my heart. I was going to do it. I just knew it.

She cried again when Matt put his phone back in his belt and said, "They should be here in about thirty minutes. I'll use the time to start looking around. I'm sure she'll be fine, but they said they're pretty full so they might have to put her out in the barn for the night."

I was going to do it. Oh God.

I made one last-ditch effort, anyway. "She'll be fine, though, right? She's like a miniature pony, and hay isn't the worst thing even if you have always slept in what looks like a pretty classy bed." I pointed at the huge dog bed in the corner with a nest of blankets, toys, and a sign on the wall over the whole thing that read PEANUT in calligraphy surrounded by a heart and arrows and doggy bones.

I was doing this.

"Can I take her?"

Gina clapped and Matt looked at me.

"I'm serious. I can't let her go to the shelter when she's obviously been pampered. At least she knows me. And it's not like Mr. Fleefers is around anyway. He probably won't even realize there's a dog there. I can put his food in another room if I have to. He likes the little room behind my closet, anyway. He hides there when he's angry with me. I guess he could do that this time, too." I shrugged and couldn't believe I was doing this.

My mom would probably love it. She loved all creatures small and enormous. I was sure she'd be able to talk my dad into it, even if he wouldn't want a dog in the funeral home, especially one that really was the size of a small pony. I just hoped my apartment would survive.

"I want something for taking her, though." I decided I'd start out big. "I want to know who Marianne really is, and I want to know what's in those files."

"Tallie, you're the one who's saying you're going to take her. I didn't ask you to do it, you're doing it all on your own."

"Then how about we look at it as Burton wants help, I'm willing to give it, but I need info?"

He shushed me. "No one is supposed to know about that."

"I understand, but I need to know what you know," I whispered.

He nodded. "I can do that. Now let's go find the dog's food, and we'll figure out a way to load all her stuff into your Lexus."

I stared at the dog. I was really doing this. I must have been crazy. It was the only acceptable explanation.

Fortunately, I was able to get ahold of my mother on the way home. I'd started out in the driver's seat, but Peanut tried to cram herself into my lap to the point where I couldn't see a thing. Gina and I switched positions. Peanut was a happy camper, woofing deep in her throat and thwapping Gina's arm with her tail. Me? I still couldn't see a thing in front of me and hoped that Gina was driving well. I couldn't worry too much about it since I was trying to keep the dog from kissing me and talk to my mother at the same time.

"Yes, Mom, she's huge. I just wanted to see if you could talk to Dad about her before I actually bring her into the building. You know, so he's not surprised to see a small pony in my apartment. He wasn't exactly pleased at the prospect of Mr. Fleefers when you let me move in upstairs. A huge Saint Bernard could make him extremely angry." Maybe this was a bad idea.

"Oh, stop. Leave your father to me. I'm so excited to meet her! I'll meet her when I come down to the parlor. Daddy will be fine!"

Daddy would not be fine, but I let it slide. "We'll be there in about five minutes." I hoped I was right. I couldn't tell where the heck we were so I could be totally wrong.

"Okay, I'm leaving now. I'll see you there. Does she need anything? A toy? A blanket? Treats?"

Peanut must have heard the last word because she started barking that deep bark that had scared me the first time. This time it vibrated the whole seat. Thank God all of my neighbors were dead. At least they couldn't complain.

We pulled into the driveway about ten minutes later. We were further out than I had thought or Gina had driven slower than I normally did. My legs were asleep from having over a hundred pounds of fluffy dog sitting on my lap. I waited for Gina to come around the car to open the door for me. Fortunately, she had the leash in hand. I rolled down the window for her to put it on Peanut while I held the dog still in case she dove for the window. She didn't move other than to wiggle in my lap, causing the tingles to start in my thighs. Getting out of the car was going to be painful.

Peanut waited while Gina opened the door and then coaxed her out of the car with a treat. The dog looked back at me, almost as if she was asking for permission. "Go, go," I told her, anticipating the pain of my sleeping legs to roar down from my thighs to my toes, which I could no longer feel.

She hopped out and immediately started sniffing around the small patch of grass behind the parking lot. It wasn't much, but she still managed to pee seven times.

My mind ran through how many times I was going

to have to walk up and down the stairs to take her out, and I groaned.

What had I signed up for?

Cats took care of themselves. As long as I gave Mr. Fleefers his food and water, and kept the little pan clean, we were good to go. Dogs were a whole different animal, literally and responsibility-wise.

But I had offered, and this is what I would do until Marianne recovered. *Please let her recover.* Quickly would be nice.

Mom zipped up in her little hatchback and was out and cooing at Peanut, who immediately licked her all the way up one side of her face. Mom's hair stood straight up above her ear, and she laughed. Okay then.

Getting Peanut to go up the stairs was another adventure. At first she wouldn't approach, and then she zoomed up the second staircase like her tail was on fire. When I was halfway up, she ran back down to the landing, then passed me again on my way up.

Mr. Fleefers must have smelled someone new in the building because he was right at the door when I opened it. I tried to grab him, but he backed up and scrambled away when Peanut came running in. He stood on top of the refrigerator while Peanut stood under him barking.

"Hush," Gina commanded, and Peanut immediately stopped barking. "Now sit." And she did.

I'd have to learn these commands and the voice to use with them.

Anxiously, Mr. Fleefers paced back and forth across the top of the refrigerator, keeping an eye on the new animal in his home. What would he do?

This could all go horribly wrong in a heartbeat. I thought of different scenarios—from Mr. Fleefers running around to the cat attacking the poor dog and digging in his wicked claws. None of them came to fruition.

Mr. Fleefers jumped down from the fridge, circled through the big dog's legs, and then sat down in front of Peanut, who also sat down. Mr. Fleefers laid down and so did Peanut, then Mr. Fleefers approached and rubbed his head under Peanut's chin. He settled on her front paws and she rested her head on his back.

What in the heck was that? It was totally better than what could have happened, but he'd never taken to anyone, or anything, like that.

I'd once brought home a goldfish from the annual street fair and constantly found Mr. Fleefers with his paw in the bowl trying to grab the poor thing. I had hoped that Mr. Fleefers wouldn't snatch it out and swallow it alive, but one day I came home and the goldfish was gone. No burial for that pet.

"Aw, look at them together!" Mom exclaimed. "What sweeties. Who knew that Mr. Fleefers just wanted a friend? You'll have to get him one after this puppy goes back to her owner."

If she went back to her owner. First, Marianne had to recover from her injuries, then she'd have to explain that wig along with her real reason for working either for or with Eli St. James. Fortunately, Matt had agreed to share it all with me.

Oh man, I should have made him write it in blood on a napkin, and sign it, then pinky swear. Instead, I'd have to take him at his word. I wish I had been able to get into those files.

Dad came up at that point and gave the dog a stare that demanded behavior. Peanut sat on her haunches right next to his leg and smiled at him. I swear that's what she did. And when he petted her head, her whole body wiggled, but she did not jump or move beyond that. I had to figure out how Dad and Gina were able to get her to behave because I was seriously failing at it.

Once all greetings were given and treats handed out in plenty, everyone but Gina left. I placed a call to Burton and left him a voicemail.

"Do you regret taking her?" Gina asked, settling onto my couch.

"No, I'm sure it will be fine for a few days." I puttered around the kitchen because lunch had come and gone and I needed to eat something. I had very little food in my fridge but enough to make some sandwiches. Grilled cheese was good for a new dog day. When I finished grilling the sandwiches and sat on the couch, Peanut was standing guard next to me looking longingly at the grilled cheese and licking her chops.

"What if it's longer than a few days? The files are bad enough but that wig is awfully suspicious, too." Gina accepted her grilled cheese, putting her plate on her knees.

"I agree, but until Matt, or Hammond, gives up the story, we don't have much to go on. At least they're going to finally look into Eli's murder."

"I think there's far more to this story than just a dead guy." She slipped a piece of her grilled cheese to

Peanut, who then rested her chin on Gina's knees next to the plate.

"Are you sure you don't want her?" I asked hopefully.

"I can't. Look at the way she and Mr. Fleefers already love each other."

Mr. Fleefers was winding around and around Peanut's front leg. Every time he came to the front she'd lick him. There was no denying that Mr. Fleefers had never been this nice to anyone, even Gina and Max, in his whole life.

Max! He was supposed to call this evening and I had a ton to tell him. He wasn't going to be happy, but it had been unavoidable. I didn't ask for any of this, but I'd see it through to the end.

I missed him and would have appreciated his cool head in all of this. I glanced over at the fridge where I had a picture of us at the annual Jubilee Day under a magnet. I wanted him to come home soon, but I hoped he liked dogs. We'd never really talked about that and we might not have to if Peanut was gone early enough.

After I ate my grilled cheese, I pulled out all of Peanut's stuff and arranged her bed under the front window, then tried to re-create the nest she'd had under her name on the wall at Marianne's. Once it was all set up, she immediately went to it and scooted over when Mr. Fleefers joined her and curled up against her side.

"Aw, look at how cute they are!" Gina said.

"Yes, very cute, but he can't get attached because this is not going to be forever."

"Right. Of course." Gina ruined it by giggling.

"Okay, let's look at what we have going on right now while we wait for a call from Burton."

"Do you really think he'll know anything this soon?"

"Burton can make some pretty quick discoveries if he's motivated properly. And Matt is giving him info on the down low since he's not officially involved."

"Okay, so what do we have?" Gina settled back into the couch and pulled her feet up under her.

"We have files in a filing cabinet that were supposed to be locked up and must have some kind of info from Eli's private-eye business. We have a woman who was at least lying about her appearance if nothing else and about not being able to access the files. She took them back to her house and then we found her beat up and spread across the bed." I grabbed a notepad from the drawer in the end table and started scribbling things down. We had far more than I had given us credit for and I didn't want to forget any of it.

"Don't forget that we have the messages on the phone, too, with the threats." Gina sat forward on the couch so far that I was afraid she might fall off.

"Maybe. Would she have had time to erase them if she didn't want anyone else to be able to access them? Maybe she took off, leaving me to look like an idiot when the cops came in?"

Finally she sat back against the cushions. "We'll have to tell Burton again about that and ask him to have Matt get the voicemails if they're still there."

If they weren't then that would be another piece missing. This case was not working out so well right now.

"If they're not there, now that Burton might actually trust me, he would probably take the notes I made on them when I listened to them." It wouldn't be hard evidence, but it would be something at least. "We also have the other inspector and Eli's brother at the borough building. I have Matt and Uncle Sherman looking into those respectively. Plus, we might be able to find those complaints that never seemed to make it past the brother. They have to be filed somewhere before they go to him. Start thinking about who you know at the borough." I gave her a piece of paper, and she started making her own list.

"This is more like it," Gina said with a grin.

"It is kind of interesting, but I wouldn't want to do it for a living. Can you imagine the kinds of people that can potentially come in as clients? Not the ones that are honestly looking for something, or need help, but the ones looking to exploit others. I think my BS meter would be swinging back and forth too much for me not to get a headache."

"I think you'd be good at it." Gina looked up from her list. "Maybe you should think about it. It wouldn't take too much schooling, I don't think. It might be something you'd really enjoy."

"Yeah, and it would put me at odds with Burton over and over again. I don't think so. There's something out there that I want more, I just haven't found it yet. I will though." I still thought about a teahouse occasionally, but that idea seemed so far away from where I was currently stuck.

"What about being Mrs. Max Bennett?" she asked.

Chapter Fourteen

Immediately my insides seized. I loved Max. I knew I did. But being a missus again might not be in the cards. I didn't want to rush things. I was fine with Gina getting married. My own situation was different. I wasn't ready to take that step just yet. Last time didn't go so well. Maybe I wasn't cut out to be a wife, just an awesome girlfriend. "I'll have to think about that. Maybe one day, but not now. So, don't go doing anything stupid like telling him to stage some elaborate proposal."

She smiled at me. "He could come to you with a calculator that reads 'Will You?' and you could sigh and hit the total button so the tape runs out with the word yes."

I rolled my eyes. "That's not even possible, Gina. When was the last time you used a calculator? It's numbers and every once in a while a word if you turn it upside down with the right numbers. I'm pretty sure will, you, and yes are not options. What about you? Are you ready to share my last name?"

"The apology and the flowers and chocolates were

nice, and I know my mom is pushing, but I need to be sure."

"Makes sense."

"Okay, enough about that. What else do we have?"

I looked at my notepad. "Lots of questions. Not a lot of answers."

Gina sighed. "And so, the part where everyone goes to do their actual jobs happens." She rose from her perch on the couch. Peanut lifted her head but when Mr. Fleefers kneaded her side she put it back down with a contented sigh. I had a bad feeling that if Marianne didn't recover, or did recover and was sent to jail for whatever she was hiding under her wig, that I had just signed on for a dog. A huge dog. For life.

Since I didn't have much else going on today, I compulsively checked in with Matt and Uncle Sherman until they both told me to stop calling every ten minutes. Matt had apologized and asked that I not tell his mom about the jail incident. He promised he wouldn't arrest me again, unless the circumstances were dire, and I agreed to keep the whole incident between us.

My wrist still hurt from my fall, so I sat on the couch with ice and my two pets, one who loved me and the other who seemed to now tolerate me because the first one loved me. We watched movies and Peanut howled every time I laughed, and laid her head on my shoulder every time I cried.

The howling would have to go as we wouldn't be able to do that when there was a funeral downstairs. Other than that, she was a peach. I couldn't deny that she added something to the atmosphere. When my mom came upstairs, she didn't even bother to ask how I was doing, or bother me about anything, because she was more interested in petting the dog and handing out treats. She'd even brought the dog a new toy and a new collar. I had to tell her that we could change it for now but when Marianne took her back we'd have to remove it. Mom scoffed and I ignored it.

Finally, the call I wanted came through from Matt, though it wasn't what I had expected. Then again, when was it ever?

"You have some time to run out to Moe's Car Corral?"

"Um, I like my Lexus just fine. It might be old, but I'm not ready to turn it in just yet."

Matt laughed and said, "I think we've found Eli's car and I think you might want to see what you can get out of Moe. He might not feel as threatened by you since you can't pull him in for anything he might be doing that's shady."

"Are you serious? Now you're using me as an informant?" I sat ramrod straight on the couch.

"Call it what you want. I just want to get some details before we go any further."

"And what am I looking for at the used car dealership?" If you could really call it that—it was more like a junker lot that Moe kept for tax purposes.

"Just Eli's car."

"Do you think Moe killed him?"

"I don't know that they even knew each other, but the car is a good place to start."

I told him I'd meet him there in ten minutes. I hurried to take Peanut outside, then made sure everyone had food and water. I told them to be good and ran out the door. Standing on the stairs halfway between the second and third floor I waited to hear any shenanigans or howling. Nothing. Good enough for me. I'd just handle whatever I came home to when I got to that point in my day.

As I sat in my car, I called Gina after remembering my promise to keep her up to date.

"Do you need me to come with you?" she asked.

"No, Matt will be there, and I'll give you the scoop when I get done. I'll call you when I'm leaving, and you can have a latte ready for me when I arrive."

"I'm not your full-service coffee bar."

"Oh, but you could be." I left her laughing, which was always a good thing.

Pulling up to Moe's lot, I looked for Matt. Eventually I spied him across the street hiding like a speed trap. He flashed his cruiser lights at me, and I got the signal. He'd be there if I was in trouble.

Moe came out of the small office with his big beer belly, comb-over, and thick glasses. He wiped his hand on a rag that he then shoved into his back pocket. Note to self: Don't shake that hand.

"What can I do for you, little lady? That's a fancy car you got there. I'll give you a song for it."

"Like literally a song? Because I already have that on the radio in the dashboard."

He laughed one of those hardy, middle-aged guy, I'm-cool-and-got-your-joke laughs. Or maybe he'd fallen for my I'm-not-the-brightest-crayon-in-the-box vibe I was trying to throw out.

"What are you looking for?"

I realized at that moment that I had not asked Matt

what Eli's car looked like and panicked. Dammit, that was the whole reason I was here, and I'd forgotten. Since I was already talking to Mow it wasn't like I could step away and call or text Matt for the information now. I'd just have to do the best I could.

"Anything new to the lot?" I tried to think what kind of car Eli might have driven and came up with some bland sedan that got good mileage but wasn't exactly good quality.

"You're in luck. Just got this in yesterday." He cleared his throat. "Owner fell on hard times and just wanted the cash, so I can cut the cost for you to something manageable if you want to turn in that beauty you drove in here with."

As I was still thinking sedan, I looked around the lot and saw that much of his inventory consisted of economy cars. Now, I was all for economy cars, and if I didn't have the Lexus, believe me I would not be choosy, as long as it could achieve freeway speeds without an issue and didn't need thousands of dollars in repairs. I spotted nothing here, though, that would make me turn in the Lexus.

"Okay," I said just to keep him on the hook.

"Come on over, and we'll get the keys to test-drive it."

I did not want to get stuck in a car with Moe and his sauerkraut breath. My mind was working furiously, but for all its effort I was coming up with no way out when he stopped in front of one of those little Smart cars. The tiny ones that looked like a stiff wind could send you careening across the road, or a truck hitting you would turn you into a pancake.

"Oh," I said trying to come off as interested yet not

thinking I had done a good job. "Where did you say it came from? It's different from everything else on your lot."

"Yes, yes it is, but I didn't want to turn the guy away. I'm sure it's a good car. Looks good under the hood, anyway, what little of it there is." He guffawed then composed himself. "Anyway, he fell on hard times. Decided to start biking to work so he gave up the car. I don't have all the papers yet, but we'd be able to work that out in no time if you're interested. I'd trust you to drive away without signing the title." His smile was big and cheesy, and I vowed never to let anyone in my family, or part of my circle, or even anyone in town, ever buy a car here.

"Can I take it for a test drive?"

"Of course, of course. Let me make a copy of your license and then we'll go from there."

Now how was I going to talk him out of coming with me? I wished someone else would show up to buy a car. Since Moe appeared to be the only one at the lot, I was pretty sure he wouldn't want to leave for a test drive if he had another potential customer.

Taking my phone out of my back pocket I shot a quick text to my brother, Dylan, the gardener. *Moe. Come quick. Pretend to buy car.*

I shot another to Matt. *Color?*

Matt texted back that I was looking at the right make of car but not the right color. I needed green and this one was red. Where was the green one then?

Dylan didn't text back right away, but I was sure he would come unless he was planting some azaleas or something. I looked over to Matt and willed him to come over. That never worked, of course.

I needed a distraction and I needed it before Moe came back with the keys.

Of all people it was my dad who happened to drive by and see me standing in the lot. He pulled in and was out of the car, headed for me with a stern look on his face, before the alarm finished beeping on his car.

"Tallie," he said in a low voice. "You cannot buy a car here. I've told you before that we can cosign a loan for you, if needed, or if you want to turn in the Lexus. So why on earth would you be here?"

I was going to joke about third-chance loans at places like this, but I didn't have enough time. "Dad, I need you to pretend you want to buy a car. I need to take a test drive by myself, and I want Moe to think he has another customer so he'll let me go by myself. Can you please do that for me? Just this once? I know what I'm doing."

"This one time," Dad said. "And then we're going to have a serious conversation about this snooping thing. If you'd come work full-time and take the partnership I'm offering you at Graver's, you wouldn't have time to be messing with things that have nothing to do with you."

Moe was within twenty feet of us, so I took a small step sideways, faced the man who had helped in my creation, and set up the performance of a lifetime, or at least my lifetime, since I didn't do things like this often.

"I'm taking the Smart car for a spin—you can find a different one."

Dad bristled and didn't miss a beat. "I need the Smart car more. I've been looking for some time and this is exactly the economical car I need. What would it take to make you change your mind?"

"Nothing will make me change my mind, I want the Smart car and you're not going to get it." I sounded like a petulant child, but Moe appeared to be eating it up.

"And I told you I need it." Dad crammed his hands on his hips.

"People, people." Moe approached with his hands outstretched. "No need to argue. I have plenty of cars on the lot."

"Do you have another Smart car?" Dad asked. Brilliant question, because I found it to be a little too smarmy that Moe had this car for only a couple of days and wanted to sell it without papers.

"Only the one."

Dad turned to walk away. "I'll find another somewhere else then."

"Wait. Wait. I do have one, but it's in the shop around back. I can bring it out, of course. Just have to warn you that it's not going to be a top performer at the moment."

"What color is it?" I said, jumping in.

"Like a greenish color?" Moe looked puzzled.

"I prefer greenish. Give this old man the red one. I'll take the other one."

Moe looked back and forth between us, and I was never so happy that I favored my mother instead of my father. I didn't chance a look at my dad because I was pretty sure he was going to be fuming about the "old man" dig.

"I think a man might be better able to handle the fixer-upper."

I saw my dad open his mouth out of the corner of my eye, but I jumped in again. "And I'll have you know that I'm perfectly capable of fixing any car. Now get me the greenish one. I'll take it for a spin and you can go with this guy just in case he has any health issues."

I left no room for discussion as Moe squinted at me. He took Dad's license and I cringed. We had the same last name. Would he notice? It wasn't like it was Smith or anything normal like that. Graver wasn't exactly common. There were quite a few of us in town and not everyone knew everyone else so it was possible I could be safe. Maybe.

Moe didn't say a word and went into the office. He left through a back door and I sincerely hoped he was going to get the other car, instead of reporting us.

When he brought the greenish Smart car around I noticed the grimace on his face, which confirmed my thought that he couldn't resist a quick sale.

This one was an olive green, like a little bug with black stripes. I valiantly did my best to gush over it. I let my father take Moe with him graciously for the test-drive and took off on my own.

At the turnoff for the Cliff restaurant, I pulled into the quiet parking lot. I wouldn't have much time and would have to be fast to find something, anything, that would be solid evidence that this was the right car. The plates had been removed and the dealer plate used magnets to stick to the back of the car. I searched every compartment, every nook and cranny. For such a small car there were quite a few. But only one that Moe must not have looked at because it held the car's registration and one of Eli's business cards. Score one for me and my investigative skills, or maybe those were just nosy skills.

I called Matt and let him know about my find. He told me to get the car back to the lot as soon as possible.

"Don't touch anything else." He sounded stern, but he was just going to have to get over himself.

"Uh, I just looked over every single inch of this car—my fingerprints are everywhere. There's nothing in here that I haven't touched. I even touched the gas tank mouth."

"Jesus, Tallie, thanks for being thorough, but you should have at least used gloves."

I narrowed my eyes even if he couldn't see me. "And when would you have had me put them on? Before I took the keys? How would I have explained that? Please enlighten me."

"Right, whatever. Just don't touch anything else and get the car back over to the dealer."

I got in and he paused but didn't hang up. "I can almost hear your own imagination overheating. Spill it. You know I'm game for whatever."

"I figured out a way to make this all very legitimate. Hammond won't know a thing."

I highly doubted that though I kept it to myself. "Spill."

And he did. I snickered as I got back into the car and tore out of the parking lot going as fast as the little putt-putt could go. I smiled when I heard the sirens behind me.

Chapter Fifteen

I saw my dad blanch through the window as he pulled up with Moe into the dealer parking lot. Moe was out of the car almost before it came to a full stop.

"Hi, hi there, what's going on, officer?" Moe stuck his hand out, and I really expected Matt to slap a handcuff on him. Instead, my cousin dropped his shades to the end of his nose, giving Moe a thorough once-over.

"This your car?"

"Uh, yes, it just came in yesterday. I didn't have time to do everything to make it salable, but this lady insisted on driving it. If she got a ticket I'm not responsible for that, you know." Indignation made Moe turn an interesting shade of puce.

"No ticket, sir, but this car has been reported stolen. When I recognized it, I pulled the driver over to see how she got it. She told me it came out of your lot, and I asked her to stick around to corroborate your story. Whatever that may be."

Moe started sweating profusely and pulling at his tie.

"Sir, how did this car get here?" Matt asked, cool like an autumn breeze.

It was almost painful to watch, but it was also fascinating to see the human mind work to spin a yarn that wouldn't immediately be thrown into the trash. You could tell the moment he came up with something he thought would fly. His face started glowing.

"Yep. So, I bought it at auction yesterday. They don't have any paperwork on it just yet, so I'm waiting for it to come to me. Yep."

As if that last yep sealed the deal.

Matt walked around the car to the driver's side to look at the car's VIN. I hadn't even thought of that. I hadn't known the VIN, though, so it would have meant nothing to me even if I had looked at it. He consulted his notebook, looked back at the number, then consulted again.

He was playing this for all it was worth.

"Why are there scratches on the VIN number? Are you buying these cars from a chop shop? We've been looking into a ring of stolen cars. If you could give me the name and the paperwork showing your purchase, I should be able to make sure this is all taken care of, and we can get you your purchase price back."

More sweat ran down Moe's face. I had a feeling he'd just painted himself into a corner that he couldn't get out of. I watched for the moment he might bolt. I wouldn't be able to take him down myself, of course, but I could certainly stick my foot out to trip him if it came down to his flight or fight instinct kicking in.

Nothing happened for a moment, and then Moe slapped his hand against his forehead. "Dammit, I knew it was too good to be true."

"What was too good to be true?" my father asked.

Surprisingly, my father could get plenty out of this guy. He knew his stuff from being a funeral director and having to talk people through all kinds of situations. He probably would have made an excellent interrogator if he'd chosen to go that route instead of following in his father's and his father's footsteps.

Moe blew out a long breath and stuck his hands on his hips. His fingers disappeared under that big belly as he lowered his head and shook it. When he looked back up, you could see more sweat, but I had a feeling he was about to tell the truth. Who wouldn't tell the truth to my father? Well, of course, except me.

"The car was in the parking lot last night with a note that said it was being surrendered. I'm not doing so good here, and it was a perfect opportunity to sell this baby. I can't seem to keep them on the lot, and they cost a pretty penny to buy off people or at auctions. I couldn't pass it up."

"And you really thought that was a good idea?" my dad asked in that soothing voice he had. The one that could sell a satin-lined coffin with nary a protest.

Moe laughed derisively. "It would have been fine if this police officer here hadn't pulled over the bird. Were you speeding around, girl?"

I didn't answer because I didn't have to. Also, I didn't want to add to the lies.

"I guess it doesn't matter." He sighed. "It was stupid all the way around. Do you have to arrest me since the car didn't sell?" Moe's face shone with hope.

"We'll talk about that later," Matt said. "Do you still

have the letter? That might go a long way toward not charging you with stealing cars."

Moe moved faster than I would have thought possible. He was back in a flash with a note.

"That's expensive paper," my dad said. "I make the high-end programs out of that. You want to talk about costing a pretty penny? You're holding about a dollar a sheet there when most paper costs less than one cent a sheet."

"Don't go anywhere," Matt said to Moe. "If I come back looking for you after I talk to my superior, and you're not here, I'm going to look at each and every car on this lot and make sure you have all the paperwork in order in triplicate. If you don't, I promise I'll shut you down. I'll also shut you down if you're not here when I call on you."

"Yes, yes. I'll be here." Moe dragged the dirty rag from his pocket across his forehead, leaving a streak of black. "Not going anywhere. I swear. I'll even stay after hours if you want so you don't have to come to my house. My wife will kill me. I have a cot in the back for when she doesn't want me around, so it won't be any different from the norm."

"You're free to go," Matt said to my dad, then turned to me. "You, come with me. I need to take you in for fingerprinting so that we can see what you touched and rule you out for being the one who stole the car in the first place."

Dad choked while Moe started sweating again. Probably knowing his prints would be all over the place. I wondered if he had wiped it down before working on it just so that no one would be able to tell who it had belonged to.

That would suck for him, but he wasn't completely blameless in this. No way had he not known that taking a surrendered car without paperwork and trying to file off the VIN were not legal.

Not my problem, but it was one more piece in the puzzle of who killed Eli.

After my brief time at the police station, where Hammond just rolled his eyes at me and sighed when I walked in, I went back to my apartment. We had a break and maybe could start finding more info now. I still wanted to know who'd killed Eli. I couldn't have everything I wanted, though. Marianne was healing, but she wasn't talking. That really wasn't my problem at the moment, except that I had her dog.

And speaking of the dog, I came home to find my mother making special dog treats in my kitchen and feeding Peanut some of the dough as she made them. Even Mr. Fleefers was there taking little nibbles.

"Oh, sweetie, hi. I didn't know if you would get home before I was done. I was going to leave you a note. Aren't these two the cutest?"

"Yes, they are." Any further conversation was cut off when my phone rang. Uncle Sherman was calling. A second break in one day would be all kinds of awesome.

"Tallie," he said before I said anything. "I don't know what you have gotten yourself into, but it took hours to find that complaint. It was hidden so deep I thought I might need scuba gear just to get a glimpse of it."

My giddiness transmitted to my mother. "Is it Max?" she whispered. "I love that he makes you smile like that!"

I didn't have the heart to tell her it was my uncle. But when she yelled hi, Uncle Sherman yelled hi back and she scowled at me. "Sherman? Is he looking into something with this stupid investigation?"

I shrugged. "This stupid investigation brought you the dog, focus on that."

And just like that a smile popped out on her face again. She hummed as she mixed something that looked like brown barf in with other nasty-looking ingredients in one of my best bowls. I'd have to run it through the dishwasher with bleach before I used it again for people food.

I walked out to the landing outside my front door, pulling the door closed behind me. I did not need her inserting comments with my every word, and I wasn't willing to deal with her right now. Plus, she had the dog and the cat to take care of, so she didn't need to pay attention to me.

Maybe this dog wasn't such a bad idea after all.

"So, what do you have?" I asked finally.

"There's a complaint, all right. Actually, there are about twenty complaints. They've never been seen by anyone but St. James's brother and the brother's longtime secretary who brought them in. The secretary who just happens to be having an affair with the brother unbeknownst to the brother's wife. It's interesting what people will tell you when they think they're about to get into trouble."

I whistled low and wondered if that was what kept the brother in check about the complaints. Maybe Eli blackmailed his brother to keep the complaints buried, and Eli got his hand greased. Eli wasn't the lackey, his brother was.

"Yeah, and there are pictures and all manner of things in these complaints that were ignored. This is going to be a huge problem in the borough, especially since some of these buildings are right in town. They are literally falling down but have passed inspection."

"Wow."

"So now that you have me on this trail, you might really want to look into the fact that one guy's wife died thanks to a faulty inspection. It said that an elevator was in prime condition in that building on the square, but it wasn't. She fell to her death. The investigation showed that the elevator was not in working condition, but they never pinned it on anyone, just a lack of maintenance."

I remembered that and her closed-casket funeral. It had been so horrible to see her husband's grief. He was inconsolable even by my mother, who was the great consoler. And what if he was the killer? I wasn't stupid enough to just go waltzing in and bring it all back up, not even for Burton. On the other hand, what if he *knew* something about who had killed Eli? We needed the info, but how to get it without showing my hand?

There was one possibility, and it was a good one— if I could get the right person to help me.

I thanked my uncle and then called Gina. She was not the person I needed, but I didn't want to leave her out. "Daphne, get the gang together in the Mystery Machine, we have a clue. Can you get away?"

"I can't. The rush is about to start. My mom can't handle that by herself. Do you want me to find someone to go with you?"

Jeremy crossed the bottom of the stairs below. We had no funerals this evening. He was the one I wanted to escort me to the house. He could come with me and maybe then he would see the importance of solving these things and giving closure. It couldn't hurt, anyway. And it would make him useful instead of skulking. As an added bonus, I'd have a reason for being at the grieving man's house.

"I'm going to take Jeremy."

"Are you sure that's a good idea?" She sounded surprised. "He might be even more against it when you're done."

"I don't think he could be any more against it than he currently is, so I have nothing to lose. I am not going to get my rear end handed to me again like last night."

"Okay, call me as soon as you're done. And keep me updated." She paused. "So, if I'm Daphne then does that make you Fred or Velma?"

"I don't know. I guess we'll see if I'm the smart one or the eye candy after this meeting."

Chapter Sixteen

Jeremy was resistant at first, almost to the point that he wanted to yell at me. The veins in his neck bulged. But Mom was the one who convinced him that I should have an escort, and as my older brother, it was his responsibility to keep me safe.

He fell for it, which was fine with me. We took his car, since he wasn't a big fan of the Lexus, and apparently he had a bunch of flowers to pick up at Monty's, the best florist in town. They were standard silk flowers that Monty rearranged for us every month or so just to keep the place filled with beautiful arrangements, or to boost the flowers at a funeral that didn't have many sprays so it would look less bare. We took a handful of the arrangements to him every few weeks and let him put them into different vases and mix the flowers up to look new.

Jeremy had Grady Jones's address in the files we kept of all the funerals we'd done over the years. As much as I wasn't a huge fan of the business, it was fascinating to look at some of the funerals from decades past.

We pulled up in front of a good-sized house in a nicer neighborhood on the outskirts of town. Unfortunately, it looked as if no one had mowed the lawn the entire summer. Dead leaves littered the front lawn and debris cluttered the front porch, which should have been inviting.

"You ready for this?" I asked Jeremy as we got out of the car.

"Yes, we're just here to check up on him after his wife's funeral last month. That is all. Whatever you ask is your own area. I'll be here so nothing bad happens, but I'm not going to be a party to that kind of digging. Maybe if you can get your answers I can get my girlfriend's time back."

So stiff. As much as I'd love to have Gina as a sister-in-law, I did have another brother who wasn't quite this unbending. Maybe I could ask her if she wanted to date Dylan. I shut the thought down before it went any further. She and Jeremy were good for each other, and it would be horribly awkward if I tried to pair her with Dylan.

"You don't have to be a party to anything. You can stay out here, and I can ask him to talk to me on the porch where you could see it all. I am here on official business for the funeral home. If I happen to ask anything else that would not be completely out of the norm."

"Don't be ridiculous, Tallie. Let's go." Jeremy headed toward the front door, leaving me at the car.

Scrambling to keep up, I met him at the porch steps and we ascended them together. A curtain twitched to the left of the front window and I got a brief glimpse of wild hair and an angry face. This ought to be fun.

I let Jeremy knock so he would be the first one the guy saw. I had said at the car that he could stay out there, but I appreciated having him here, even more than having Gina by my side. Two women against one angry man could go horribly wrong. One man and one woman could, too, but at least this way we had a legitimate reason for being here.

"What?" Grady said after yanking open the door. The fumes of whiskey radiated from him, so much so that I had to hold my reflexive gag back.

Jeremy stood in front of me, appearing to be completely unaffected. "Grady, how are you? We at Graver's just wanted to see how you were doing."

"I already paid my bill, get off my porch."

My brother was not deterred. "Thank you for paying in full. We appreciate that. This is the other side of our services, making sure the people we serve are checked on."

"I don't need you to check on me, you and your sister." He sneered. "All perfect with your perfect lives and all your family standing around, making money off the dead. Vultures, all of you."

Jeremy did not blink, or flinch, and I was awesomely proud of him. "My apologies for intruding on your continued grief. Just know that we are all thinking of you. I wanted you to also know that if you need anything we're here for more than just burying your loved ones."

"How about getting me that no-good liar who said the elevator was fine? I told him he needed to take more than two minutes to look at it, but he wouldn't do it. I told my wife not to take the elevator down until

I could find someone more reliable to go over every aspect, but she was in such a hurry one day, so she took the elevator and plunged to her death. In my building. In my elevator, on my watch. I killed her more than anyone else, but since I'm paying for it with every breath I take I want him to pay, too. Dammit."

His speech made me feel hollow inside. The poor guy. To deal with that level of grief. And yet there was my opening. I took it, hoping I showed as much compassion and kindness as Jeremy had. "We are so sorry for your loss. Would that have been Eli St. James that did your inspection? We have recently heard some things and they are looking into the inspections he's done to see if anything hasn't been done correctly."

That seemed to sober him right up. He stood tall, dragging a hand through his hair. "I'm part of the reason they're looking. I asked Jeremy if I could come out with him on his visit to talk to you about what you remember so they can build the strongest case possible. Eli is dead at this point, but he and his estate could possibly pay posthumously."

"Dead?" He squinted at me.

"Yes."

"And you're here because you wanted my story?"

"If you want to share it."

"I just did. Are you sure you're not the cops and you think I killed him? Eye for an eye? Life for a life?"

Now I could have pretended to be a cop here and taken some sort of statement or told him that we were looking at all suspects and all cases. But I felt for this guy, and I just couldn't do it. "I'm not with the cops. I'm looking into it because I don't believe he died of natural causes. I don't think you did it, but I offered to talk with you to keep the cops out of your business."

"Huh."

And that was it. He shut the door in our faces. We could hear him clomping away out of the foyer.

"Should we stay or go?" Jeremy asked.

"Song references, brother of mine?" When he looked confused, I just rolled past it. "I'm honestly not sure. I don't want him to come back with a gun and tell us to get off the property again, but I also don't want to be halfway down the road if he was just going to get something and didn't want to leave his door wide open."

Before we could make a decision, Grady whipped the door back open. I wasn't lying when I said I was afraid of a bullet. But what he shoved at me didn't have a barrel. It did, however, give me a wicked paper cut.

"That's everything I found out about the guy. He had some shady stuff going on. I was working on stuff myself, but I can't anymore. It's destroying me. You let me know what you find out about his so-called work and I'll be there to make the case as strong as a lockbox."

He closed the door again. Definitely for the final time. Jeremy and I walked away to the sounds of him sobbing on the other side of the door. My eyes teared up, but I held it in until I got to the car and we were halfway down the street.

Jeremy pulled over and held me across the center console as the tears flowed, unchecked. "Tallie, it's okay. It means he's going to be okay, and you're doing something to make that happen. You were really good back there. I know you don't want to hear it, and you don't want to do it, but I think you would make an amazing funeral director. You weren't only born into it, you also have all the personality traits that make you a natural."

I didn't say anything because I didn't know what the answer was. Besides, I wasn't ready to face that my calling might not be my call.

Back home, I leafed through the papers in Grady's file as I waited for Max to pick up on his end. It was the middle of the workday, but I needed to hear his voice and I needed his advice.

"Babe, how's it going?"

"I miss you a lot," I said with a smile in my voice, but there might have been tears in my eyes. Maybe.

"I miss you, too. I should be home a day or two early and was going to just have them change my flight to Harrisburg so I can rent a car and come visit. I'll drop the car off at Dulles afterward and pick up my car from there."

"You really are the best." I wiped my eyes, moving Peanut away before she howled.

"Depends on who you're asking. The company here is not overly impressed with my investigative skills, since it just landed them in hot water with some people farther up on the chain."

"Very nicely done."

"I won't bore you with the details. How are things? Did they find the murderer?"

"Not yet, but they did find Eli's car, and it looks like he might have been playing private investigator to get money out of people. Not to mention shoddy home and building inspections to do the same."

"Yikes. That's a lot going on. How are you narrowing things down?"

I sighed and flopped back against the couch cushions. "I'm not. That's the problem. I have Rhoda, who it might be. I have Marianne. I have Grady, even if he said he didn't do it. His wife was killed in an elevator Eli signed off on as being safe. He's angry but I don't think he did it. I do appreciate that I now have a multitude of other possibilities from the info Grady compiled. But then there are all those other files that Marianne had. So the suspect pool is currently Olympic-sized."

"Well, I feel better that you have Burton on your side this time."

"Yeah, he's not being much help, but at least he's not scowling at me every time I get near him while warning me away. He's actually asking me to help."

"I wouldn't count on that lasting beyond this particular case. You know he's going to go back to his usual self as soon as he's back on his feet."

"I wouldn't be surprised. In the meantime, I'd better get moving."

"My amateur sleuth. Just remember I'd prefer you alive."

"Me, too."

We were about to end our call when he said, "I know you have people on your side, but I really wish you'd wait until I got back to do anything more with this. I would feel better if I was there to back you up. Jeremy's fine and so are Burton and Gina, but I'm better."

"Yes, you are, and hopefully this is the end of my involvement. I just have to turn this paperwork over to Hammond."

"As soon as possible," he cut in.

"Yes, as soon as possible. Then I'll let them handle it. I'll be fine. Promise."

"I hope so. I'd hate for this to be our last conversation. I can only imagine how that Grady guy feels."

Wow, that struck a chord. How would I feel if Max never came back and I knew who was responsible? Horrible, that's how I'd feel. And it made me want to hug Max close as soon as possible.

"We'll discuss that, at length, when you get home. Hurry."

"I'm on it."

I was counting on that.

The next morning, I couldn't resist at least peeking into the file before I handed it over to Hammond. What I found gave me a full list of people who could have wanted Eli dead. Most of them were homeowners who had filed complaints. I didn't know how Grady had gotten them, but he must have dug around, or gone to demand them from other people who had been burned by Eli. Those I had already given to Burton from Uncle Sherman. I flipped past those fast enough to get to the other, more personal, things.

One stood out in particular, and that was one of his rivals: Mick O'Rourke. Apparently, they had originally been in business together, but Eli had split off, taking the business and all the money, leaving the other guy to rebuild with nothing.

Mick lived two towns over, and it was easy enough to set up an appointment with him. He had never returned my call from the other day, and with Marianne's assault and everything else that had happened I had forgotten to follow up.

But when I wanted an appointment, he was quick to get back to me. Fortunately he did free consultations so I wouldn't have to pay for it out of pocket. I gave him Jeremy's address to inspect for a possible sale and then let Jeremy know I was going over there. When he asked why and I told him, he offered to come with me, just in case. Since we didn't have any funerals this afternoon and Gina was still working I accepted his offer.

I looked around the internet and took Peanut out. Poor baby was in desperate need of a walk. We only had so much grass around the paved parking lot with the two hearses, and she kept straining against the leash. After she peed several times, I decided to take her out to the inn and walk along the creek. If I happened to find any clues we'd just call it a bonus. Mr. Fleefers had not been happy to be left at home, but he'd just have to deal. The one time I'd tried to put a leash on him, he'd played dead for about thirty seconds, then jumped up and dug his claws into my leg. That was not happening again.

I set out in the Lexus and parked it in a turnaround at the edge of the woods bordering the inn's property. I didn't want to bother Rhoda or Arthur. I wasn't sure what to make of Rhoda not wanting to believe Eli was murdered.

At this point there had only been two people in the house that I knew of, Rhoda and Arthur. I couldn't imagine that either of them had killed Eli, despite what Annie had hinted at. But I wasn't ready to face them and have them lie to me either. I had anticipated a call to clean but hadn't heard from her yet about cleaning after everyone left. She'd promised to use me, so I wasn't worried. The call would come. She might have been caught up in booking visits now that the inn was reopened and there'd probably be a message for me to come by soon.

Call me a coward, but I did not want it to be either of them.

In the meantime, I had a dog to walk.

I got out of my car with my rain boots on. Even though it was a dry day in fall that did not mean it couldn't get wet quickly. And the threat of ticks also had me in jeans and a jacket. With any luck I'd be in and out pretty quickly before anything attached itself to me.

Walking along through the woods, I took the path carved out by four-wheelers that liked to come back here. I made sure to keep an ear out for any of them coming up behind me. I heard the roar of their engines throughout the woods and kept mindful of stepping in one's path.

Honestly, I had no idea what I was doing out here except that I hadn't wanted to go to the park, and I needed the quiet to work through the pieces I had currently. Not that I had many. I had files of people he'd screwed professionally, those he was trying to get money out of for both business and pleasure. And he must have been able to help at least some of the people in those files for his private-eye side business, otherwise why did anyone go to him?

Birds flew through the low-hanging branches, singing their afternoon song. Rustling sounded on the ground and I stepped back onto the path. Not everything that lived out here might be happy that I was invading their territory.

Nothing flashed at me, no signs pointing and saying "here, here's where the murderer ran away to!" I kicked a rock and kept going. I heard a splash and figured I was close to the creek bank. I'd have to be careful. There were definitely snakes and whatnot that made their home here and I didn't want to see them any more than they wanted to see me. Mr. Fleefers I liked, Peanut was growing on me, but my love of animals did not necessarily extend to the wild kind unless I was watching them through a window or on some internet video being cute—not within my personal space.

I kicked another rock and waited for it to hit the water. It did—and something else splashed along with it. Something bigger and heavier. Before peeking over the edge of the overhanging bank, I tied Peanut's leash to a nearby tree. I wasn't sure what I'd find, but I certainly wasn't expecting to see a man's blank stare.

I'd found another body. And he was not looking nearly as clean as Eli had, though he looked very similar. Eli St. James's brother was no longer going to bury paperwork in his office at the borough. We were probably going to bury him in one of our coffins.

Chapter Seventeen

I was not leaving the body. The decision wasn't even one I had to think about. I'd been made a fool of once and I was not going to be made a fool of again. Hammond would have to do some serious fast talking to make this look like it wasn't a murder.

I snapped a picture with the camera on my phone, though I felt gross doing it. He wasn't bloated, which meant he was killed recently.

I heard an engine roar to life and wondered if the murderer was getting away. I debated running after the noise, but there was no way I was going to catch the person on foot, and it made more sense to stay where I was. Or did it? The person on the four-wheeler could always come back and try to run me down.

At this point I just needed to get the authorities out here and make them admit Eli had been murdered and that I hadn't been hallucinating.

Of course, cell service out here sucked. I waved my arm up high to see if it would make a difference, but it didn't. Dammit. I was not leaving the body behind. The last thing I needed was to have found him and then either have something drag him away or for the creek to decide to dislodge him from the bank.

How was I going to do this?

I tried sending the picture via text to Burton with a message about finding the guy. The police station didn't exactly have a cell phone number I could call. I also tried emailing the photo to the police and Gina with a disclaimer about what it was before anyone opened the attachment. My phone said they went through, but I was doubtful. When I tried to call Burton the call would not connect. Thank goodness I didn't have an emergency out here.

I needed clearer skies and less trees. I considered climbing one of the oaks and seeing if that made a difference, but in the end I had to do what I dreaded. I waded into the middle of the creek and watched the body from the water that didn't even come above my rain boots. See? Why was I scared of the water? Nothing bad was going to happen for wading out to the middle.

My call went through this time. When Burton answered he sounded groggy but there was nothing I could do to help it.

"I found another one."

"What?"

Yep, decidedly groggy. I hoped he wasn't on pain medication that would make him forget this conversation.

"I found a body, Eli's brother to be precise, down by the creek, he's tangled up in some weeds or something. I didn't check anything, but I know for certain he is dead. Can you call the police and ask them to come down here?"

"Tallie. What am I going to do with you?" Now he sounded far more awake.

"I was trying to take this monstrous dog for a walk and sort through the facts."

I turned around in the water to give Burton some idea of exactly where I was and spotted Peanut trying to gnaw her leash off the tree I'd tied her to. The last thing I needed was for her to get loose and romp around in the forest. There was no telling where she'd go or how I'd get her back.

"Burton, I have to go. The dog is trying to get loose and I'm not having her run nor am I leaving the body. Have someone come down here ASAP."

"Fine. But don't touch anything."

"Do you ever get tired of saying that?"

"You're the only one I've ever had to say it to, so, yes, I get tired of saying it to you. If you'd stay out of things I might never have to say it again."

"I'll remind you that you're the one who got me in this time. If people would stop doing bad things, I might not have to get involved."

"Touché. I'll call the station and have someone down there soon."

"I'll be waiting."

And wait I did. Since I hadn't been able to give a precise location and the woods were big, I'd told Burton to have them find my Lexus, go to the creek bank and just start heading south.

Matt found me first. I met him on the bank with Peanut at my side.

"Jesus, Tallie, I can't keep doing this."

"Where's Hammond?"

"He was out on a call so I'm it for the moment. I

have to call this in to tell people where to find us. Don't move from this spot."

"As if I would."

Gina texted me back and yelled at me to which I replied that I had been walking the dog and did not go searching for this.

She sent me a picture of a macramé potholder. I texted her back that I did not need a freaking hobby.

"Tell me everything." Matt stood next to me looking around.

"I was walking Peanut and I heard something on the bank. When I looked I found the body and then I heard a four-wheeler engine start up. The person took off but with the trees I couldn't tell in what direction."

Matt's face tightened and he made notes furiously in his notebook.

"Did you touch anything?"

"No, not even the dead body. From the weeds and the blank stare, I figured there would be no pulse, so I didn't try to even get close."

"Well, at least there's that."

Another engine sounded in the forest, but this time it was an ambulance carrying Hammond. He gave me one look after getting out of the back of the ambulance, grunted, and walked away.

"Not a big fan," I whispered to Matt.

"None of us are."

I didn't have time to ask if he meant not a big fan of mine, or if we all weren't big fans of Hammond's.

Hammond stayed far away from me, even going so far as to beckon Matt over instead of coming to where we stood on the bank.

"Are you going to want a statement?" I yelled, and Peanut howled.

"What Matt has is enough. You can leave," Hammond yelled back, and Peanut howled again.

I wasn't going to argue with that. I had to look over my list of people again and find out why the two brothers were dead. Was it the scheme with the taxes? Had someone finally gotten fed up? Had someone wanted in on the action and the two had stonewalled him? Why bring the brother out here to kill him instead of somewhere else?

If nothing else at least this put my mind to rest about Rhoda or Arthur being the killer, even if it was very close to their property. Rhoda never came out here—she didn't like the forest. And Arthur couldn't make it out here. Neither of them drove a four-wheeler. They didn't even own one. So, two off the list, thankfully, but who had just made it onto my short list?

I'd been sent home after the police had secured the scene. Not having to answer any other questions left me at odds. I passed Annie on my way out of the woods and she hadn't even waved to me, just turned her face away in disgust.

I went by the Bean and Gina gave me a coffee. Back at home, I called my mom's cousin, Velma. She worked at the hospital where they had taken Marianne. Maybe I could get her to give me some personal information so I could see if there was a next of kin who might want a huge dog. Peanut was growing on me, but the apartment felt smaller and smaller every time I walked in.

Velma had nothing to say except that Marianne had had a visitor who claimed to be her husband. I asked to be notified next time he came in. Who was this guy and was it true? Why hadn't she mentioned a husband? Where did he live? Was he involved? Why wasn't he looking for his dog?

As I thought about what to do next, my phone rang.

It was Velma. "I know I shouldn't tell you this, but the husband just showed up. He tends to stay for about thirty minutes. Get down here now." She hung up.

I let Gina know where I was going and asked her to take Peanut back to the apartment so I could get to the hospital. Mama Shirley shook her head, but there was nothing I could do.

I was careful to stay just under the speed limit so as not to draw attention to myself. I still made it to the hospital in record time since for once the lights worked in my favor.

Velma snagged me as I reached the third floor.

"Don't go storming in. Let's at least get you into a candy-striper outfit so it makes sense for you to be in there."

I had worked as a candy-striper for community service hours in my senior year to graduate, but not since then. I couldn't remember what they did. And why did I have to have a disguise when Marianne, or whatever her name was, would recognize me the second I walked in anyway?

But I played along. Velma wouldn't let me near the room unless I did.

I donned the apron and let Velma tie it around my

waist. Pulling my hair back into a ponytail, I pushed a cart in front of me to collect trash. Another cleaning job. At least this role I didn't have to stretch myself much to ace.

In short, I felt ridiculous in my red-and-white-striped pinafore, but when I saw the cop outside the woman's door, I was very thankful that Velma was able to lead me right in as her assistant.

Peeking around Velma, I scoped out the scene. Marianne was in the bed, hooked up to monitors, looking wan. She reached out to a man who sat to her right. When Velma entered the room, he turned and looked up.

I identified him instantly from looking at his picture on the internet. This was the man who had been Eli St. James's partner before Eli had run off with all the assets and their business: Mick O'Rourke.

Marianne clapped her hands on her head as soon as I cleared the door.

"Oh, dear, oh dear, oh dear."

"Marianne, you know Mick?" What in the world was going on? Was this her freaking husband? No way!

"I, um, well . . ."

"Is Mick your husband? How many other lies have you told me?" I propped my hand on my striped hip.

"It's not her fault," Mick said.

"I've been looking *everywhere* for answers for her. I've taken her dog in. I talked with my uncle about her unpaid rent. It might not be her fault, but from where I'm standing she's not exactly innocent, is she?"

"I'm so sorry, Tallie. I didn't mean for any of this to happen."

I didn't care. I just wanted to get out of here with my feelings of betrayal. But I couldn't leave before I got what I'd come for. "I'm not here for anything but some answers. Another body was just found so you couldn't have killed both of them, but I want to know if you killed Eli."

I wasn't sure if she'd say anything at all. As time dragged on, her husband put his hand on her arm to encourage her to tell her story. Or at least I thought it was her husband. They had different last names unless she'd changed hers. But Velma had said he called himself Marianne's husband. I was going to go with it since I didn't have any other information.

"I've been working for Eli to get his secrets and hopefully get my husband's business back. We had been so good, all of us together, but then Eli got greedy and left and took everything with him. It wasn't fair."

"Now, honey, there was no need to do that. I was working on it through the legal channels. You risked a lot in case he had recognized you."

Marianne snorted. "He wouldn't notice."

"Is your real name Marianne?" I had to know so I could add her to my list of search engine searches.

Her husband closed his eyes and she clamped her lips together.

"The police are going to want to know. I want to know, and Hammond is going to come looking for you now that Eli's brother is also dead. You had files that most certainly did not belong to you in with your *Better Homes and Gardens* magazines."

"The police." Her voice shook as she said that last word.

"You have nothing to fear. So you took some files," her husband said. "In light of the current situation, I'm sure that's small potatoes compared to two un-explained deaths."

Marianne's mouth trembled. Was there something more going on here? From the info Matt had given me, she wasn't talking about who had hit her. She refused to speak about it or when asked simply said she hadn't seen anyone. Why?

She had to have seen them coming, let them in. Per Matt's information, there hadn't been any damage to the front door, no forced entry. So, she must have let whoever it was in. She didn't appear to be afraid of her husband, so I doubted it was a case of domestic violence.

"Who beat you up, Marianne?"

She shook her head.

"Who beat you up enough to put you in the hospital?" I asked more forcefully. "I have to know if you want me to help you. You know I've already done a lot for you, from helping with your rent situation to taking your dog so she didn't have to go to the pound while you're in here. Tell me who did this to you."

Her face turned green, and the heart monitor in the corner of the room went haywire.

"Hammond," she whispered, just as the room was overrun with three nurses and a physician's assistant. Velma waved me out of the room behind her back and I took the cue.

Hammond had roughed her up! Now he was mine. I would be able to go to Burton now, and with some more information maybe I could figure out who had the most to lose in Eli St. James's files or the most to gain by his death. Did he have a file on Hammond? Was Hammond working with him? Was Hammond the one who'd gotten greedy and had taken Eli out? So many possibilities.

Scrambling out to my car, I sat in the front seat and placed the most gleeful call to Burton.

"Hammond?" he crowed after I dumped my info on him.

"Yep. And then her machines went haywire. That might be why Peanut kept howling at him every time he spoke in the woods. She knew who he was."

"But he has a solid alibi for Eli's death." Burton sighed. "I can have him pulled in for assault, but I'm not going to be able to get him for the murder."

"At least not the first one," I reminded him. "He could have killed the brother. He wouldn't come close and his hair was wet. Maybe he hadn't just jumped out of the shower. Maybe he'd been tussling with the second victim in the creek to get a file. Or all the files."

"I like that. If nothing else, I can have him kept in holding while we figure things out." He paused and blew out a breath. "I might regret saying this in the future, Tallie, but good work."

And now it was me who was crowing. *Good work, Tallie.* I liked those words immensely.

"I told you I didn't deliberately find him, Max." This was the third time he'd cautioned me against looking into these deaths. To be honest, I was tired.

"I'm not saying you deliberately found him, but I'm asking you to deliberately stay out of this."

Should I tell him about Burton's request? Was it still even valid now that the police had no choice but to look into Eli's death, and now his brother's, as murders? It could have been possible that Eli had a heart attack and fell very neatly and precisely onto a bed at an inn where he was not supposed to be. But there was no way to explain the brother also dying not a hundred yards away in the creek. He had not accidentally fallen in. His neck was broken and his lungs were not filled with liquid. My dad was the acting coroner at the moment and actually shared that piece of information with me without me having to beg for it. Go figure.

The coroner who had signed off on Eli's death had been pulled in for questioning. I so wished I could be a fly on the wall for that one. But that was not to be. My dad had started that whole process when Eli's body was released to him and he was able to very quickly confirm that the coroner had lied on his report. The man's neck was broken, no doubt about that. He might have also had a heart attack, that would take longer to determine, but his neck was most definitely broken and it wasn't an accident. Dad didn't go so far as to apologize to me for doubting my word on the cause of death, but he did take the opportunity to tell me I would be invaluable in the business if I could spot a broken neck from outside the window. I highly doubted that. I still gave him points for trying, even if it wasn't swaying me to take him up on his offer.

I hoped that Matt would honor his word to keep

me informed about the coroner and the deaths. Speak of the devil and he rang.

"Babe, I have to go. Matt is calling."

"Keep me updated and please stay safe."

"Will do."

I pressed the screen to disconnect with Max and picked up the next call.

"Yes, cousin of mine."

"I need you to meet me in the blue parlor. I'm downstairs waiting for you."

He hung up and I looked at my phone. Why were we meeting here and why was he already in the building?

No way to find out but to run down the stairs. It was more of a trot with a stumble or two, but no one could see me except me, so I didn't worry too much about it.

Until I got to the bottom of the stairs.

My father stood with his arms crossed over his chest. "I agreed to the dog and can even handle the barking for the moment, but I will not tolerate you running down the stairs like a herd of elephants."

Matt stood in the doorway of the blue parlor with a slight smirk on his face. My God, I was tired of being treated like a child.

"Dad, I love you, and I appreciate you wanting things to be the way you always saw them, but I can't continue to work with you and live here if every single thing I do is a disappointment to you. Think about that, and let's talk some more later."

Did I just invite him to lambast me more? Maybe he would let up instead. I wasn't holding my breath, but I was going to see Matt. Now.

I breezed past my dad and shut the door behind me, forcing Matt to back up.

"Was that smart?" he asked.

"I don't care. He keeps trying to convince me to join Jeremy in running this mausoleum and I'm not going to do it if I never do anything right."

"I get it. It's one of the reasons I'm not throwing pizza down the street."

I peered at him. "I thought your father didn't want you to throw pizza and wanted more for you than to work in the service industry."

Matt snorted out a laugh. "That's the story my mom tells so my dad can save face. I didn't want to make pies. I wanted to make a difference." He crossed his arms over his chest. "And now I need you to help me make a difference, too."

I should have liked the idea of helping to make a difference, but to say I was leery would have been an understatement. "I'm listening."

"I need you to go back and talk to Marianne. She won't talk to us—she won't even let us into her room, and since we don't have any evidence that she did anything truly wrong just yet, I can't force her hand. See what you can find out."

Baffled, I stood there with my mouth hanging open and my hands on my hips. What alternate universe was this? Had I laid down to take a nap and didn't realize I was sleeping? With my hands clasped behind my back, I pinched the inside of my wrist and barely resisted the urge to yelp. Real and very much awake. First Burton and now Matt asking for me to play mole. What was next? Uncle Sherman wanting me to run point on the next fire?

"And what am I supposed to use as a reason to go back and see her? I tried asking her name and she clammed up. She gave me Hammond's name already. What makes you think she'll share anything else?"

"Because you're going to say you stole these back for her and see if she'll trust you enough to tell you what they are and what they mean."

As he thrust a stack of folders out at me, I kept my hands very firmly behind my back.

"Do you think Hammond killed both of the St. James brothers?" I asked.

"I don't know, but I need to before anyone else does. I know this is a lot to ask, but I have to."

He thrust the folders at me again and this time I took them.

"No, no, it's fine." I'd started browsing the folders and was shocked at some of the names I found in the files and not shocked at all at some of the others.

But if Marianne had killed Eli, then who had killed the brother? She had been in the hospital so she couldn't have done both, unless she and her husband were a team of killers, which I'd come across last time I'd been embroiled in one of these things.

Believe me, I wasn't ruling it out, but it didn't feel right. Of course, it was very much a possibility, but I needed more time to think. First, I had to look through these files.

Gina came over with sticky buns and milkshakes. They were not going to do anything but make my hips bigger. But since I loved them, that was fine with me.

"So, what have we got?" she said as she curled up

on the couch. Peanut rested her head on the couch at her knee and Mr. Fleefers curled right into her lap. I was abandoned at the kitchen table, so I decided to join them on the couch.

I brought the folder and a notepad with me. Balancing the paper on my knees, I flipped open the folder and stared at a page with a photo of a man who looked familiar. "This one is looking for his birth parents because he's sick. He doesn't want a relationship with them, just medical information, in case it can help with his treatment."

"Aw, poor guy. Does it say anything about the birth parents being found?"

I searched through the stapled pages and came up with nothing except some chicken scrawl and some initials. Were they the mother's? Someone else's? A person of interest?

Come on! If Eli had thought these were secrets then why couldn't he just have written the people's names down, for crying out loud?

I turned the page to show Gina and she snorted. "Not going to be that easy, is it?"

"Of course not, Daphne. And I've decided I'm going to be Velma minus the glasses. Now, let's dig in." I handed her half the pages. We systematically went through the cases—some sad, some ridiculous, some smarmy—but none that clearly pointed to why Eli had been killed. Maybe the cheating wife could have been a victim for the hate mail Eli had received for not moving fast enough to prove she was stepping out, but I didn't think the author of the letter would kill the guy who was keeping tabs on his wandering wife.

The wills and the way people wanted others to be proven unsavory to make themselves look better were a little hard to stomach with the lies Eli had put in the columns. He clearly stated he could make up and support these lies to tear the other person down. But no real names, just initials or first names like Jane and John. Was there a code book somewhere? What had Marianne been looking for in the files? And what had she hoped to do with them? Use them to take up where Eli had left off?

My mom's cousin, Velma, was off shift but Matt had made sure that I could get in to talk with Marianne in thirty minutes. I shut my last file and looked at Gina. "Anything?"

"A couple of things that are interesting. I bet I could figure out who these people are if we know the geographical area. Was Eli only operating around here or on the internet, too?" Gina snapped her fingers. "You know what? Mama Shirley could probably glance at these and tell you who every person is. She is the main hub of gossip and has been around a long time. There doesn't seem to be anyone she doesn't know."

"Brilliant! Take them to her while I go to the hospital. We'll talk after we've both accomplished our missions."

"Should we synchronize our watches?" She laughed and I threw a pillow at her. Peanut did not take kindly to that and barked at me with her teeth bared.

"Hey, sorry, okay, sorry."

Gina put her hand on Peanut's head and the barking stopped immediately. "You go do your thing, and I'll do mine. 1800 hours and we're back here."

"Is that five or six at night?"

"Six, Tallie, and you'd better get the lingo if you want to be an international spy."

I picked up another pillow to wing at her, but Peanut eyed me. I put it down so as not to rile her again.

"Fine, we'll meet back here and compare notes. Do you need anything else?"

"Nope, just this and the notepad. Go find out what Ms. Wig knows and what she was planning to do with it."

I saluted her, then walked out the door, leaving my animals behind.

I'd be back soon enough and then maybe we could finally get some answers. And not more questions.

Chapter Eighteen

"You need to be straight with me, Marianne. The cops want you, they want you bad, and they think you followed Eli to the inn and then killed him when he wouldn't let you in on the action." Not the truth, but she didn't need to know that. Matt had asked me to gain her trust, but I was going a different route. I'd tried being nice to her and helping her. This time she was going to answer my questions. Honestly.

"I swear to you I didn't hurt him, I barely knew him."

"That's not the truth. You did know him through your husband. And he is the one who took your income away and ran away with it to set up for himself, making far more than you and Mick had with those kickbacks. Tell me you didn't start working with him in a wig to find out what he was doing and how to get a piece of it for yourself."

She started crying, but I wasn't buying it. Even if they were real tears I needed to know why she was crying. Was it because she'd killed someone? Because she'd gone much further than just keeping tabs on him and trying to get her husband's business back?

"Yes, I wanted to know what he knew and I wanted to punish him for what he did to Mick, but I swear I didn't kill him. I wouldn't even know the first thing about killing someone."

"Not in a moment of revenge, irritation? Maybe you went to the inn when he told you he had a meeting and decided that this was the perfect time to make him tell you things. Then, when he wouldn't, you strangled him, or broke his neck."

She choked. "No, no I would never do that. I swear to you."

"Then where were you?"

"I was in the office. I can show you the calls I made. Yes, I was trying to use the files to make money for myself. I had started calling the people being investigated and telling them that Eli was looking into them and then offering my services to get him to stop."

"And how were you planning on doing that?"

"I hadn't thought that far yet, and no one took me up on the offer. But ultimately, I wanted to get those complaints from pissed-off people sent through the channels to make sure the right people saw them. I wanted Eli out of business, to make him pay with disgrace and financial ruin, not dead. Dead meant he'd never have to pay for his crimes."

That made sense. Mick chose that moment to come into the room. He narrowed his eyes at me and headed for the door, probably to tell on me for being there, when Marianne stopped him.

"Honey, don't. I told her my part in this. I don't want to make it worse. Maybe she can help us figure out what happened. I know why Hammond hit me, because he wanted his file, but not the rest."

"And what was in the file?" I asked.

"I really don't know. I didn't look in it." Her eyes were downcast and I knew a liar when I saw one, but I wasn't sure how much I could press. If I could just get my hands on the file then I wouldn't have to deal with her again for information.

Mick sat, holding his wife's hand with his eyes still narrowed. "And what will you get in return for this?"

"Honestly, I'm happy to get the satisfaction of taking Hammond down a peg. I was tired of his high-handedness. And now he's behind bars, but they're not going to be able to keep him if I can't find the file and if you won't tell the police your part in this. I'm not going to press you for what was in his file because I need proof. Without the actual paperwork, I can't go to the police. I need more than hearsay. But if I have the file and can solve these murders, then I not only get to see him behind bars, but I get to see him squirm for not having outsmarted a 'troublesome amateur' as he called me."

"And we get closure." Marianne squeezed her husband's hand and he grunted.

"Fine, but Marianne does not get in trouble for any of this," Mick said

"I can't make that promise," I told him. "She did steal the folders out of Eli's office and stuck them in her basket. I don't know what she'll get for that. But I'm sure it will go a whole lot better, faster, if I can bring in the killer and keep the spotlight off her."

He didn't grunt again but his face became thoughtful.

"And do you think my chances of actually getting to do home inspections around here will go up? I hardly ever got calls out here because Eli bad-mouthed me to everyone before and after he became a code enforcer."

I had no idea, but I felt that it wasn't necessary to tell him that. "I'm sure they will. Especially now that his brother is also dead, I think those complaints are going to go through and the public will find out how many people he screwed, both as a home inspector and more recently as a code enforcer looking to be bribed. Maybe you can clean up by doing honest and truthful assessments." Though I wasn't sure about that either since he had worked with Eli before. Did they have the same kind of character? Had Eli once been good at his job then got greedy and took his show on the road? "So, tell me what happened to your partnership."

A measly fifteen minutes later I got kicked out of the room so that Marianne could take a shower. I needed more time but the nurse who came in was having none of it. I had more questions, the biggest one being what had Hammond done to have a file? There wasn't much I could do if Marianne wouldn't tell me or would continue to lie about knowing what was in the folder. Maybe I would have to come back and get some more answers once I could figure out how to get her to tell me the truth.

In the meantime, Mick walked me to the elevator. "You talk to that Burton guy and tell him to keep Marianne out of this and we'll give him a statement."

Was he implying that he wouldn't make a statement if Marianne got in trouble? I didn't think it worked that way. Fortunately, it wasn't my business. "I'll do my best. Go take care of your wife. I'll do my part to see this through."

Taking the elevator to the bottom floor, I used the time to contemplate how everything would come together. Hammond was on the hook for several things but still not Eli's murder. Or at least that's what I thought. So, I had pieces and parts of the story but not the whole. What was I missing?

So many avenues and no map. I was going to have to draw one, and I knew just who to handle the marker. I dialed her number as I walked to my car.

"Daphne, meet me at the apartment. We have a murder board to draw."

I was halfway to my car when Marianne's number popped up on my phone.

"I'll get right back to you, Gina." I hit the call receive button. "What's up, Marianne? I thought you were in the shower."

"I told them to wait while I made this call. There are things I didn't tell you. It was definitely Hammond who hit me, and it's because he wanted his file."

"You told me that."

"But I didn't tell you what was in it."

"I noticed that, but I was going to ask when I came back. So hit me with it." I hesitated with my hand on the door of the Lexus.

"Hammond isn't just shady, he is downright evil.

He and Eli were in league together. Hammond had come into the office a couple of times, and during the last visit they were screaming at each other. The walls muffled the words but I do remember that Eli was supposed to pay him for the information. Eli had been unhappy with the information he'd gotten about some kid, so he refused and Hammond went ballistic. Eli calmed him down somehow. I saw the file, Tallie, he's got sidelines on drugs in Chambersburg, looking the other way and has lied to get criminals off because they pay him."

"And no one has turned him in?"

"No one but Eli had proof. That's what kept Hammond in check. That's why Hammond wanted the death to be a heart attack because he didn't want anyone to look into it."

Now we were getting somewhere.

I had note cards and markers and string. I had seen this in a few movies. I'd put everyone on the board and use string to connect them. Maybe I had been watching too much TV, but I was not getting a hobby to replace that, either.

We had Marianne and Mick; Grady, the guy whose wife had died in the elevator accident; the brother; and a number of homeowners. But I didn't have all of them, so they were more of a cluster than individuals. After forty-five minutes I saw no way to loop the string except that the brother would have been involved in every single one of the houses with the taxes raised or lowered depending on the amount of grease given. The chicken scrawl on the kid's file had only revealed he was looking for medical information because he was sick. If there had been blackmail, I had a feeling that had all been on Eli's part. But I still couldn't get anything more than the initials of the person.

"Crap." I paced away from the refrigerator where I had used magnets to keep everything together.

"Now, don't go getting pissy, but you didn't put Rhoda and Arthur up there," Gina said.

I whipped around and glared at her. "Rhoda did not kill that man, why would she? And Arthur has a hard time getting out of bed by himself. He gets around fine in the wheelchair, but Eli was not short and there's no way Arthur could have taken him down, broken his neck, then placed him neatly on the bed. I just don't believe it." But I knew that my justifications were weak.

"Mama Shirley said that a few years after Arthur and Rhonda married, she went away for a year, and when she came back she was sad. Mama heard through the grapevine that it was an affair that bore a child. Initials are 'R.M. '—Rhoda Monroe."

A child? "Adoption?"

"According to the tales, yes. She gave the baby up because it wasn't Arthur's."

"And they still stayed married? They never had any children of their own."

"Arthur was willing to raise the boy, but Rhoda didn't think she'd be able to look at him every day and not think about her mistakes."

That was a different Rhoda than I knew. But, really, how well did I know her? She was a friend of the family. Someone who baked wonderful bread, which

meant I didn't really know anything about her inside
landscape.

"So, what do I do? Go talk to her to see if Eli was
blackmailing her and came to get money? She killed
him because the inn was reopening and she wanted to
make sure it was pristine?"

It sounded far-fetched. The problem was Matt had
called and there was absolutely no way Hammond
could have killed Eli. His time was accounted for in
the police station logbook, and Suzy had grudgingly
vouched for him. I'd heard it was quite the scathing,
nasty vouching, but a vouching nonetheless.

I didn't feel much better about Rhoda as a suspect
when Gina shrugged her shoulders.

"You're the one who does the deducing in this
whole thing," she said. "I just bring you the facts and
flip my hair while looking cute."

"Where's your Fred tonight?"

"He has a meeting with a new client and then we're
going to hang out. But he told me to do whatever I
needed to do."

Of course he had, because my mother had probably driven into his head that he wasn't going to be
able to keep someone as awesome as Gina if he re-
verted to a Neanderthal.

"Okay, so should I talk to her now?" I looked out
the window where Peanut was resting her head on the
ledge. Mr. Fleefers had taken up residence on her
back. Despite speaking with Mick and Marianne earlier, neither had mentioned the dog. Maybe they were
having a hard time dealing with the mess they'd created. Maybe they didn't want to think about her until
they could get her back. What did I know?

I did know that I wasn't sure if I wanted to give her up just yet. There was enough time to worry about that when Marianne was released from the hospital.

"I think tomorrow is soon enough, and now, with the new murder you might want to lay low for the night. Talk to Max, see what he's doing, maybe have a little sexy talk and then go to bed. You'll figure it out tomorrow and I'll be right there with you."

"You're going to go with me? I'm not sure that's a good idea since I don't want you to get hurt."

"I don't want you to get hurt, either, and we're better as a team. I can sit in the living room, or even the car, while you talk if you want, but I'm not letting you go out there by yourself. And that's final. We should go in the morning since people will be checking in that afternoon. I don't know if they'll have a hostess to check in with, but that's not our problem."

And she latched onto my elbow in case I had any doubts that she was serious. So, we'd do this in the morning. Together, apparently.

I headed to bed with my mind full of how I was going to deal with Rhoda tomorrow. I did not want to confront her. I didn't want it to be her. But I had to face the fact that it could be, and if it was I'd have to turn her in. My stomach clenched at the possibility, but I'd do it. I'd have to.

Pulling the Murphy bed from the wall, I climbed in. And was promptly joined by Peanut and Mr. Fleefers. I half-heartedly shoved at Peanut because she really shouldn't be on the bed. And once Max was here, she definitely wouldn't fit. But she wasn't

budging, and maybe I wanted her up there to hold on
to. My heart hurt for Rhoda and especially Arthur.
Not to mention Annie was going to have a fit that I
was coming for her boss and the woman who was a
mother figure to her.

I closed my eyes, hoping that I could just sleep and
deal with it all tomorrow. I also hoped that someone
else would pop into my mind as the true culprit. It
had to be someone else. Had to be!

My mind floated in that fog of almost asleep when
my phone rang. No more calls. I didn't want any more
information or tips or lies.

But then I sat up quickly, dislodging Mr. Fleefers
from around my head and barely bothering Peanut,
who was blissfully snoring away.

Scrambling out of bed, I made a dash for my
phone. Maybe this was the real culprit. Someone who
would confess all so I didn't have to go see Rhoda
tomorrow!

"Hello?"

"Tallie, I'm going to need you to come down to
the station." Burton sounded angry. At me? No, I
hadn't handed him a killer yet, but he did have Hammond and that was worth something as far as I was
concerned.

"Right now?"

"Yes, right this instant. Do not dawdle." And then
he hung up on me.

I guessed I was going to the station. At nine thirty,
for heaven's sake, I realized when I glanced at the
clock.

Putting on a pair of sweatpants and a hoodie, I

called myself done. Burton could just take me as I was if he was going to demand I come as soon as he called.

As I turned out of my driveway, I glanced at Gina's windows and found them dark. This was just the police station and nothing was going to happen to me there. I wasn't going to bring her with me this time. I'd fill her in on all the details tomorrow.

The ride was short but filled with me talking out loud to myself.

"What on earth does he want?" I asked the side mirror as I pulled out onto Main Street.

"Am I going to be in trouble?" I said as I drove slowly past the funeral home front.

"Should I have worn something different if they're going to throw me in jail?" I pondered as I made a right turn.

"Nah, at least I'll be comfortable in these sweats." Since I was now answering myself I thought it was a good thing that I pulled into a parking spot at the police station.

The place wasn't quite a zoo when I entered through the double doors, but it was close. Suzy was giving out orders like she owned the place, Matt leaned against the far wall with a big smile, and Burton paced across the industrial carpeting, only stopping when he looked up and spotted me.

"Well, at least no one will be able to see you," he said instead of a greeting.

"You didn't exactly tell me what I was here for and you're lucky I didn't just come in my pajamas." I stuck my hands into my hoodie pocket and crunched in on myself. Who would be here this late to see me anyway? And what was I doing here?

"Follow me." Burton took off down the hall toward the dreaded interview room. Suzy scrambled behind him as fast as she could after she forwarded all standard calls to the answering service for the moment and made Gary sit at the desk.

Gary was not happy to be missing the fun, whatever that fun was, but Suzy pulled the seniority card and he did it even as he grumbled about her not even being sworn in. She yanked my arm to lead me away even as she lifted it to smack him in the back of the head. "We don't have time for this. I don't want to miss anything!"

I still had no idea why I was there as Suzy dropped my arm and nearly ran down the hallway. Matt sauntered along behind the crowd, that big smile still on display.

"Care to tell me what is going on, dear cousin?" I sauntered with him since it might be the last thing I did before I got in trouble. I wasn't going to hustle toward a cell if Burton was going to try to force me into one.

"Oh, you'll see, and you're going to love this." His stride was lazy, his arms swinging in time with his step. He held a folder I desperately wanted to get a peek at, but I knew better than to ask.

I highly doubted I'd love anything about this station.

However, I had been wrong before, and I was wrong now.

Matt stood casually at the interview room door while Burton led Suzy and I back to the little dark space to the left. I'd sat in that interview room a few days ago with Hammond, not knowing if I was going to get out unscathed as he demanded I only answer with one word to each question. Just thinking about that made me happy he was somewhere in this stupid place, hopefully locked up with no coffee or water and wearing an orange jumpsuit.

But this was different. This was the other side of the two-way mirror. I would be the one looking in. But at who?

Burton opened the door for us from the hallway then waved his hand for us to go through. "You have to stay in here," he said. "And don't interfere. We're going to throw you under the bus in there, Tallie, I'm just warning you now."

"What?" I demanded.

"We're going to see if we can't get him to crack by using you as a hammer."

I gripped my hands tight in front of me. "Won't he come after me, though?"

"No, when we're done with him, he won't come after anyone ever again."

"You promise?" I couldn't help shaking in my shoes. If Hammond got off and then tracked me down, he could do some serious damage. Witness what he'd done to Marianne just to get a file. This was his whole life and I'd be right in the middle of his sights.

"Promise." After pointing to two chairs in the twilight-like darkness, he put his finger against his lips. "Be good, Tallie, or you won't get to see it all."

"Of course." Like I needed the warning. Despite my worries, this was better than any movie or television show I'd ever seen. Or at least I hoped it would be. Like Gina with her thinking that we were just going to solve the mystery in a day and run around looking for a guy in a mask, I had high hopes that this would be dramatic. However, also like Gina and her mistaken idea of how things went, I, too, could be disappointed.

Were they bringing Marianne back in for more information? Had they found the killer and not told me? Maybe I wouldn't have to confront Rhoda tomorrow.

And then I looked through the window and saw Hammond in all his angry glory. Oh my word! Where the heck was the popcorn?

I'd heard earlier that they had brought him in wearing his uniform, but someone must have busted him down to civilian clothes. No orange jumpsuit, which was a bit of a disappointment, but I'd go with it.

Either they'd gotten the clothes from his house or he was borrowing someone else's. They didn't look like they fit him, though. So maybe he'd been outfitted with borrowed clothes. I could live with that. For what he'd done, he should have everything stripped from him. Not that I wanted to see him naked, thank you very much.

He sat in a chair, his back rigid and his icy eyes narrowed, his fists clenched on the scarred wooden table before him. His blond hair was slightly tousled as if he'd been running those meaty fingers through it.

I recognized the back of Matt's head and waited to see what would happen.

"I heard they found a file in his house," Suzy whispered.

"Can they hear us on the other side?" I whispered back.

"No, but I want to make sure I don't miss anything they say. This guy has been a jerk since he got here, and I cannot *wait* for them to take him down like a cheetah with a wounded warthog."

"Warthog?" I snickered. "That is actually a very apt description of him." If he'd had some tusks to go with the fierce scowl on his face, I didn't doubt he'd snort.

"Now, shh, Matt just put the file down on the table. I want to see what they're going to go after him for first." The absolute glee in her voice transferred to me and I gripped the edge of the window sill in anticipation.

Only Matt and Hammond sat in the room. I wondered if Burton was coming in later to be the bad cop or the worse cop.

"There's quite a few things in here that you're going to want to answer for." Matt's voice came over a speaker, sounding tinny in the small room. Those words, though, were like a volley off the starboard side of a pirate ship or a gauntlet thrown down on the ground.

"I'm not answering to you." The icy eyes were still narrowed but now Hammond's nostrils flared too. Seriously, Suzy was right on the mark with that warthog reference. His fists clenched until his knuckles turned white. I had a brief thought that I hoped he would reach over the table and clock Matt, but I had to trust that the police at least knew how to do this part of their job right.

"I strongly suggest you think about that, Hammond. Burton's mad enough to let me do the interview because he's not certain if he can contain himself. You don't want me to bring him in here."

Hammond snorted, for real, and it was almost

beyond my ability to hold in my snicker. Suzy smacked me in the arm and shushed me again,

"You can throw whatever you want at me," Hammond said. "I'm not going down like this. There are plenty of people who will vouch for me. You have no real evidence, just a bunch of crap from a dead guy who swindled people out of money, stupid people out of their stupid money. So, bring it on. Whatever you have. And we'll go from there. Because I guarantee you I'll get out of this, and then I'm coming for your job, and I'm taking Burton to the wall."

Those were fighting words in my book. As further proof that I was right, Suzy tensed next to me.

"Oh, I really hope Burton was getting a cup of coffee when Hammond said that." Suzy leaned forward in her chair. "I do not want him in there."

Personally, I thought it might look a little like a cage match, and I was up for that.

"Hammond, you have no idea what you're up against," Matt replied in a scathing tone. "It's not just me and Burton you need to be worried about. Our friend Tallie found a few things on you that are proof. Absolute proof. And they will absolutely put your rear end in jail for long enough that you'll be hunched over and gray by the time you get out."

Suzy and I looked at each other as silence filled both rooms.

"What did you find?" Suzy asked, just as Hammond roared almost the same phrase.

"Nothing that I know of," I answered Suzy, watching Hammond throw back his chair and stalk around the room. Matt was careful to keep his eyes on the man who really did look like a warthog about to charge.

"That piece of interfering trash is going to pay. What did she find? What does she think she's going to be able to do? Did Darryl talk? I'll get him too. Did Teagan spill his liver? If they think for one minute that I'm going to go down for those things myself, then they are going to be hurting." He paced from the window to the door like a caged animal.

"Both talked and a whole lot more. We know all about the games you've been playing in our borough and several others. Nothing's secret anymore. They all sang to Tallie like she was the sweetheart they were trying to woo."

Now I was the one snorting. That was taking it a little too far. I was not exactly woo-worthy. But Hammond didn't seem to notice.

Hammond slammed his fist into the wall next to the door. The door Burton entered through with his tie completely straight and his angry face on.

"Uh-oh," I whispered to Suzy.

"Shh, just watch."

"You're going to want to sit down, Hammond." Burton chose the seat next to Matt. I wasn't sure if he was going to be the bad cop or the worse cop yet, I'd have to wait and see.

"I will not sit down. Whatever she has on me is a lie. All of it. That's all she does is lie and interfere and get mixed up with other people. It was supposed to be so simple, and then she came in and tripped over the freaking answer to everything that's been holding me back."

"Tallie has a way of doing that." This from Burton. Maybe he was going to be the nice cop? Not to me, if he was going to keep giving me backhanded compliments, but at this point I didn't care.

"She shouldn't have been there. I was supposed to go talk to that lady at the inn. I was the one who found out about the kid. But then St. James got greedy and it all went to hell."

"It usually does when she's around," Matt said. Apparently, it was bash Tallie hour in the interview room.

"Did you drop Eli's car at the lot?" Burton asked.

"No, it was already gone that afternoon. I didn't care at that point. All I saw was that my trouble was over. I could finally get back to doing what I was supposed to be doing." The paneled wall at the back of the interview room must have been fascinating, because Hammond's eyes didn't move from it, and he kept tracing the grooves with his index finger.

"And you don't know who moved it?" Matt asked.

"It could have all been so simple. Eli was dead, just like I wanted him to be, but I couldn't do it myself. It could've been a heart attack. I had the coroner sign off on it and everything. But she just couldn't leave it alone." He picked another groove and ran his finger along it.

"I'll tell you one thing, she's tenacious. That's why we also know you killed Eli's brother."

They did?

"How do they know that?" I whispered to Suzy. "And how did I have time to do all this?"

"Just watch."

Burton opened the folder, tapped his finger on the

top page a few times, then closed it when Hammond came to look.

"I didn't—"

Burton just shook his head, lifted the folder, and opened it again to where Hammond couldn't see it. "Pictures, Hammond. Lots of pictures. You set this whole thing up to be your own downfall. You should have been nice to Tallie when she first said it was a murder. You should have at least pretended to look into it, and then put her off. She might have bought it and let you fake doing your job. Maybe she would have gotten involved in something else and forgotten about it. But when you pissed her off on that first day you unleashed a ferocious terrier."

I did not particularly like being compared to a small dog. I would have preferred the magnificence of Peanut.

Burton was still talking, though. So, I tuned back in.

"And when you unleashed that terrier, you led her around by your scent. She might not have known exactly what she was looking for, but then you gave her a dog who didn't like you after you hit her mistress. A dog she was walking in the woods when you drove away on your four-wheeler after choking Eli's brother to death and leaving him in the creek. The same four-wheeler that's sitting in your garage with its muddy tires."

Dang, I wish I had been that smart.

My respect for Burton rose exponentially as he talked calmly with Hammond, who finally broke and admitted to killing the brother but not Eli. He hadn't cared who'd killed Eli as long as he was dead.

Several times he came back to the fact that he'd been looking for the mother of the sick kid. And he'd been at the inn to find her. So, I guess I wasn't getting out of talking to Rhoda tomorrow.

Had this all to do with one man who only wanted medical information? I'd taken a picture of the chicken scratch and sent it to Max, who had deciphered a little for me. The guy didn't want to reunite with his birth parents. He didn't want a relationship. He'd just wanted a medical history so that the doctors could look into how to cure him.

The child that Eli had tried to ask Mrs. Koser about. The one in the file with only initials. Had the mother killed Eli? Was the mother Rhoda?

I didn't know if I'd be able to sleep tonight, but once Burton came out of the room and asked if I'd seen enough I told him I had.

"So, if I'm smart enough to do all that stuff, according to you, then next time will you just let me help from the beginning instead of roadblocking me?" I asked cheekily.

I got a stern face for my efforts.

"There won't be a next time, Tallie. Now go home and go to bed."

The next morning, the inn stood in all its stone glory back from the road. I must say I was proud that the windows still gleamed.

It was the inside I was concerned about. What would I find? How was I going to talk to Rhoda about a possible baby she gave away during her marriage to

Arthur? It wasn't Arthur's from the grapevine's info, and that would only make this more uncomfortable.

My only hope was that something good would come to me and I wouldn't just blurt it out.

I left Gina in the car, demanding that she stay like a dog. She grumped about it, but she had offered to come here, and this was close enough. I did not want to embarrass Rhoda even though I could essentially be asking her if she was a killer and an adulterer. Her comment on that first day about always keeping things in order rang in my head. Had the murder been to keep things in order? Her life intact? Had Eli tried to blackmail her and she'd gone ballistic to keep the life she'd worked so hard to perfect all these years?

I could not promise her that she would get off for the murder so I'd skate around that and give it to the police to work out once I had confirmation that it was her. Though at least she hadn't killed the brother. Hammond had done that.

I'd never gone in before without a clue as to what I was doing, and I did not like it this time. But I had a handy trick in my pocket. Literally! Burton was on speakerphone in my shirt pocket. I'd thought about my back pocket but didn't want to sit on him.

"Going in," I said under my breath. Hopefully he heard me. I had made it so I couldn't hear him but he could hear me. Actually, I'd made Gina's nephew tell me how to do that since he was far more tech savvy than yours truly was inclined to be.

Knocking on the door, I heard Rhoda yell out for me to come in. She had no idea who it could be and a serial killer might be on the loose. Was she so confident that it would be no one who would hurt her since she was the killer?

"Let the show begin," I mumbled. I pushed through the door and sucked in the delicious smells of sugary goodness baking. I was surprised she was wrist deep in dough when this was the grand reopening day, but maybe this was how she worked out her stress and the rest of the setup was already done.

"Tallie! What brings you by? Come give us a hug!" Rhoda smiled over her shoulder with her hands in a bowl again. Had those hands broken a man's neck who was not exactly a kind soul but one who hadn't deserved to be killed?

Jailed? Yes. Killed? No. Especially if it was only to keep her secret. And the poor kid didn't even want anything from her except some medical information.

No one had to know unless Eli had been trying to blackmail her about the child she'd given away.

I hugged her shoulders and stayed away from the bowl. To do anything else would have been suspect before I was ready to lay out my cards. I still hadn't come up with a brilliant way to introduce the subject of her being a killer. "Thought I'd come by and see how you're doing. Annie has stopped at the Bean a few times to let me know this whole thing has you distraught. I wanted to see how you were handling things."

"Oh, fine. Of course it's sad that that poor man drowned in the creek, but those waters can be more dangerous than anyone gives them credit for." Taking her hands out of the bowl, she moved to the sink and washed them thoroughly. Once she was done she went for the block of knives and my heart seized in my chest. She was going to double her body count! I should have brought Gina in. When would I learn?

Rhoda turned around with a towel, drying her hands, and I took a breath.

"Something wrong, dear? You seem upset. Do you want a cookie? A muffin?" Her blue eyes were wide and caring behind her thick glasses, but that didn't mean anything.

It was, however, an opening. Maybe not the best one, and maybe I was just going to blurt it out. I had Burton in my pocket and Gina in the car, and this woman wouldn't get the drop on me.

"So, there's a story going around town that made me think that you and I should talk." I sat at the center island in the kitchen. Picking up a salt shaker shaped like a hedgehog, I rolled it back and forth between my fingers.

"Aren't there always stories going around?" She chuckled. "Is this the one where the inn is tanking and I am selling? Or the one where we're up to our eyeballs in debt? Or the one where I use frozen food instead of making everything myself? My sheet thread count isn't as high as I say it is?" She laughed again.

"Um, no, this is the one where you had a secret love child and you'd do anything to protect that secret."

I watched for her fists to clench or her shoulders to go up, her hand to reach for something to use as a weapon. I had not done that subtly, or right, probably, but I had to know.

Her hands stayed flat on the table and her shoulders hunched forward, she reached for nothing as tears slid down her face.

Dammit. It was true then, she had murdered Eli, and I was going to have to turn her in. This amateur sleuthing business wasn't always about turning in a bad guy who you were more than happy to see suffer, and it sucked.

Chapter Nineteen

I waited for Rhoda to say something, but she just kept gulping and looking at her hands. Had she strangled him? But my dad had said his neck was broken, so she must have had such strength in those fingers and anger that she didn't know her usual limits. From kneading bread?

And then she did reach for something—a napkin. She blotted her face as we sat in silence, and I waited and waited. I didn't quite know for what. Previously the people I caught had been angry and ready to try to kill me for finding them out, willing to give me their evil monologue as they tried to end my life, too. But Rhoda just seemed broken and sad.

Me, too.

"It was during the war. Arthur was deployed and I was so lonely. I thought he was never coming back, and we had a terrible fight before he left. I wanted him to muster out. He wanted to fight in some god-forsaken jungle. I thought I wasn't important. But he didn't have any choice. I wasn't looking at it like that. So, he left, and I went to a dance in town and walked home with a boy who was at the local base. He came around a few times and we . . . you know . . ." Under her tears a blush formed.

I took pity on her. "I know."

"When Arthur came home I didn't know how to tell him I was pregnant, but I did and told him that he could leave and I would understand because I had broken our vows." She sniffed and I wanted to sniff with her, even though I knew she and Arthur were still together. They must have worked it out somehow. "He told me that things happen, and it was a test that we might not have passed the first time, but we'd make it right from here on out. That was forty years ago, and we made it."

And now I was going to have to turn her in and put her in jail for the rest of her life at sixty-five.

I wish I had never come.

"But then when I was six months pregnant, I fell down the stairs and was rushed to the hospital. The baby didn't make it. I loved that little one and Arthur had agreed to take him on as his own and raise him with all the love we had for each other. We never did have any more children. I think it was punishment for the things I did wrong."

"Wait, what? The baby died?" I gripped the edge of the island until my fingers turned white.

She dabbed at her eyes again. "Yes, there was no way to bring him back after that fall. They let me know that he was gone, and I cried and cried. Arthur held me through it all. Promising me that it wasn't a punishment. But he was wrong, and now the whole town will know because that stupid man Eli tried to blackmail me for something that wasn't even true!"

"And that's why you broke his neck when you thought no one was here?"

This whole time she'd never looked at me. She'd looked at her hands and far off as if lost back in time but not at me directly. Now she zeroed in with a precision magnified by her big thick glasses.

"What are you saying?"

"The police know that Eli was blackmailing people, and he wasn't supposed to be here that day. He called his secretary to tell her he had a business meeting he forgot and came to the inn. He told you he wanted money from you and then did you tell him to go to one of the rooms and you'd discuss it? The man who was asking for the information only wanted his medical history. No matter what Eli told you, the client didn't want anyone else to know he was here. But if the baby died, then that can't be your son."

The kitchen door creaked and we both looked over our shoulders.

Maybe Gina had decided to come in anyway. But it was only Annie. "Oh, you have a visitor. I'll talk to you later then."

"This won't take long, hon. Tallie and I are just finishing up. Come back in about ten minutes or so."

"That's fine. I have some things to tend to in the barn, anyway. Paul went to the store for those blueberries you wanted."

"Excellent, thank you, dear!"

Annie left without glaring at me again. Maybe she finally understood that things were coming to a head. I knew she wanted to protect the woman she thought of as a mother, however, this had gone further than one killing.

Unfortunately, that left me with a crying Rhoda and no solid lead of where to go next. I had been so sure it was her who was trying to derail me from investigating anything and lying to the police about knowing he was here. And maybe she was still lying. Just because she said the baby had died didn't mean it actually had. She could just be revising history so she didn't look guilty.

I could go to the police with what I had and let them handle the rest, but I didn't believe it would be taken care of at this point. They had their hands full with the mess created by Hammond being a dirty cop. Given that he had beat up Marianne to get her to stay quiet should land him in hot water for years, preferably in a prison. And if that didn't put him there, then certainly his admitting that he'd killed Eli's brother would put him away for life. When I'd set up this scenario with Burton, he'd told me that they'd found the file on Hammond, which he so desperately wanted bad enough that he hit Marianne to keep her quiet. Hammond would have killed her if my precious Peanut had not tried to rip the rear end of his jeans off to get him away from Marianne.

While there was no evidence of murder, just his statement, which should be enough, there was plenty of paperwork showing his pursuit of power over the town, and the underhanded things Eli had found out about him to get him to work with him.

So, the question then was should I just leave?

"I should go," I said to Rhoda. "I'm sorry for bringing up such sad memories. I just want to solve this mystery."

"I know, dear, and I have been trying to wrack my

brain for who it might be, but I have nothing. Perhaps one of the other people? There were three other cars in the drive that day, and there shouldn't have been any. Eli's and a maroon hatchback, as well as a turquoise sedan. I did find out that the one belonged to the caterer who was talking with Annie, and the other belonged to the helper Paul was interviewing, so I guess that leaves them out."

I guess it did. Back to the drawing board.

I left Rhoda in the kitchen and listened to her sob for just a few seconds. I had brought the grief on again after all these years, but I had to be sure it wasn't her. It was tempting to go into the private residence and see if I could talk with Arthur. Maybe he was the one who had actually killed Eli. The man who would stand by his woman through anything and had seen combat might have lost it when his life and his wife were threatened. But I still struggled with how he would have accomplished all that from a wheelchair.

I turned to go back to talk with Rhoda again when something slammed into the back of my head. I went down like a ton of bricks.

I woke up sputtering for the second time in a week. This time my head was in the water, not dripping with dirty water from my bucket. I had no idea how much time had passed, but it was enough that I was no longer where I had fallen and I was dripping wet.

It took me a moment to orient myself. How could this be?

And then I realized I was in the creek and someone

was shoving my head back under the water and trying to drown me.

I struggled and fought as best I could, but whoever it was had strength like I couldn't imagine. They held me down and light burst in front of my eyes. I held my breath as long as possible, but it was getting harder not to open my mouth and scream. Especially when I saw a fish swim by my face and a snake float by. My God, I was going to die and sleep with the fishes.

And then air, precious air as I made one last futile attempt to resurface and kicked whoever it was in the shin or some other part that startled the person enough to let go.

I scrambled back on my hands like I was doing the crab walk in fourth-grade gym. At this point, I didn't care what was in the water with me as long as I was still breathing. I hit one of those dips in the streambed and stumbled, almost drowning myself, but shot up out of the water just as a branch came at my head. I ducked and sidestepped and finally was able to see my attacker.

"Annie?"

"You just do not know when to stay down." She growled and came for me again, her Victorian dress dragging through the water at her knees.

"What in the world?" I backed away from her, scooting my feet along the ground to make sure I didn't hit another of those dips. She was too close, and she was between me and the bank. I could have dived for the other bank but it was a steep cliff and there was no way I'd be able to get away. At least not without her hitting me, or dragging me back to the water.

I had to get around her. Preferably before she swung with that stick again.

Keep her talking. It had never worked for me before but maybe there was a first time for everything.

"I don't get it. What was Eli after you for?"

"As if you don't know."

"Um, I don't, or I wouldn't be asking."

She laughed, and it was tinged with a maniacal twist that frightened me more than the snake that skittered two feet away.

I felt my pocket for my phone and found it gone. No one was going to save me. If Burton wasn't listening and Gina was obliviously sitting in the car listening to music and Rhoda was baking her bread and dreaming of the child she never had, and Max was across the country, then no one was coming to save me. I'd save myself, dammit.

"Is the child yours?"

"You don't know? I'm R.M. My first name is Rhiannon and my maiden name was Matthews. I heard you ask Rhoda about that."

It clicked in my head. Annie was a nickname for Rhiannon, but she wasn't the right age. Was she? And she said she couldn't have children in the coffee shop that day. The coffee shop where first she'd tried to get me to drop the whole thing, and second she'd tried to blame it on the woman she said she thought of as a mother.

"The child is mine, and so is the shame of getting pregnant out of wedlock to a man who couldn't do the right thing. I was not going to pay one penny to that lowlife Eli, though. I knew he was coming for me next if he found Rhoda. He wouldn't be far away from finding me. I was so careful to cover everything up and I never told Paul. He still doesn't know. It was before we got married, and he didn't need to know since the deed was done. I went away for six months, faked a fight with my parents, and told them I needed time to sort through my life before I started to show. And then I had that little brat and gave him away to the first family who would take him. And now he comes back to haunt me. I did the right thing. I did and now I have to pay for it again and again. Well, I wasn't going to do that. And so my secret is safe. You didn't figure it out, and no one else will."

"The police already know."

"No, they don't, Tallie. Don't try to pull that crap with me. I know everything you know, you and your little friend, who by the way is taking a nap that hopefully she might wake up from even though you're not going to survive your impromptu swim."

I looked down as if checking out my attire when really I was searching for a weapon. Any weapon. "In my jeans, in the fall? You really think the police are going to believe that?"

"They don't need to because I'm going to blame it on Hammond. He was down here, too. He's the one who killed that brother of Eli's, and I have proof. So, I'll throw him under the bus for both."

"Why would he have killed me, though?" She must not have known that Hammond was in jail, and I wasn't going to be the one to tell her. I was still trying to circle around her, but she kept matching me step for step, so I couldn't get around her. We were going to be in this godforsaken creek forever if she had her way. Or at least I would. The water had started creeping up her dress, absorbing into the layers of petticoats and velvet until her steps started slowing. Not by much, and she kept walking as if she didn't notice in her fury, but I had, and I was waiting for that dress to get too heavy. I just had to survive until then.

"You are a menace and should have gotten a hobby. You don't need to involve yourself in affairs that have nothing to do with you."

"Is that what you had? An affair and that's where the baby came from? You know your child only wanted to know about his medical history. The blackmailing was all Eli."

She closed her eyes and inhaled. When her eyes opened, I was fifteen feet away and halfway to the bank. Who knew I could be that fast?

"Just the medical information?"

"Yes, he didn't want anything from you. He's dying and he needed his medical information to see if they could find something in his background to look at that might help."

"He's dying?" she repeated, her expression flat.

"He is," I answered softly

Her eyes closed again, and this time I moved in a different direction. I wasn't going to be able to leave her in the creek and go get help before she took off, even in that dress. I had to subdue her and get her tied up. But with what?

And then I saw it. Fishing wire tangled in the branch above me. People often fished here and with the branches so low, they often didn't cast right. They'd cut bait and walk down a little ways in their waders to a clearer spot and leave the line in the trees. And that was my ticket to freedom if I could get it.

As quietly as I could, I stepped around her and yanked on the fishing wire. It wasn't quiet, though. It didn't matter because she was crying and she probably couldn't see me through the flood of tears. Heaving sobs dropped her to her knees in the creek. The water came up to her chest, soaking the dress and pulling at the lace on her sleeves.

"Dying. I know I called him a little brat, but I loved him and I wanted to keep him. I just couldn't when I got no support. In the end, I tried so hard to give him the life I wouldn't be able to give him, and he's dying."

I kept my mouth shut. I didn't want her to look over at me as I grabbed the tree branch and used my weight to try to snap it off the tree. Bouncing a few times made it creak, but it wasn't enough.

"Everything is for nothing. That damn Eli, I'm glad he's dead. He was trying to get Rhoda to pay to keep her secret and it wasn't even hers."

Keep talking, girl. One more bounce and the tree limb came free in my hands. I fell into the creek again on my rear end this time but scrambled up.

"And just what in the world do you think you're going to do with that?" she asked, her voice low and menacing again.

I had been afraid this was going to happen. Now that she'd cried, she was pissed and was going to take it out on me. The time for action was now. I'd have to swing this tree limb and hit her hard if I was going to save myself, but it made my stomach hurt to think about hurting another person.

"Stop right there."

We both turned to see Burton standing on the bank, gun drawn. Max stood next to him, and I almost dropped everything to run to him. Annie did drop into the water and tried to float away down the creek, but her dress only pulled her down and sank her where she sat on the creek bed.

"It's over, Annie. Give up," Burton said.

"You bastard!" Annie screamed.

Max, Burton, and I all looked at each other since I wasn't sure who she was talking to.

"Your brother couldn't do the right thing, and look where all this got me. Drowning in a river and looking at a life's sentence for a child I wanted that he wouldn't step up for!"

Oh. Now we all looked at Burton. His face was a blank slate as he kept his gun trained on her. He stepped into the creek to the crying woman. Since she'd lost the stick in the current, I stepped closer in an effort to help him.

She came up with a rock in each hand. She threw one at me and tried to nail Burton in the head with the other one. He was faster, though, and not as wet. He tackled her, crying out as he used his injured shoulder to take her down.

And that's how Rhoda found us.

Rhoda took Annie into her room to get her a change of clothes. Burton stood in the doorway with his back turned but not willing to leave her alone.

After that he took her to the station and Max took me home. Gina followed in my car.

Without talking about it we all decided to meet at the Bean.

I wanted caffeine and sugar, but first dry clothes. I

said hi to Peanut and Mr. Fleefers, changed, and then ran back outside. Marianne caught me on the sidewalk.

"You're out." I wasn't sure what else to say. She hadn't been without some blame in this whole thing, but I had no idea what Burton would charge her with, if any.

"Yeah, just for a little while. There was a quick hearing and I'm on probation for the moment. If I slip up again I have to go to jail." Her blond hair was so much more her and I wondered how I had missed that in the first place.

"So, don't screw up." I shrugged and realized that she was probably here for Peanut. My heart clenched. While I hadn't wanted her in the beginning, I didn't want to let her go now. But it was probably for the best because I really didn't have the room to keep a Saint Bernard. It still made me sad, though, and Mr. Fleefers was probably going to be a pain in the butt with the crying when the big dog left.

"I'm not going to. Mick and I are going to move to another state to start over again, just to get out of here. This place is quite the secret keeper."

"We're not that bad, just like any other group of people."

"Except for the murderers."

"Oh, um, well I guess there is that, but maybe this is the last one."

"Yeah, well I won't be here to watch. But that leads me to my precious Peanut."

She was going to ask for the adorable dog back. Who knew I would feel this attached to her when I'd only had her for a handful of days and hadn't wanted her in the first place?

"I can go get her and all her stuff. She's just right upstairs." I gulped.

"No," she said softly. "No." She swiped a hand under her eye. "I'm sorry I never asked about her while I was in the hospital, but I just couldn't. It hurt too much to think about her, so I didn't. But I knew in my heart she'd be safe with you. And now, I want to ask you to keep her. I don't know where we're going to end up, and I can't have my Peanut living in a car. She's too lovely to be dragged all over the country. And who knows what our finances are going to be now." She grabbed my hand and squeezed. "Will you take care of her? I can give you my roaming vacuum cleaner to deal with the shedding."

"I . . . um . . . of course." Not that the roaming vacuum cleaner was the deal clincher. I did not like those things.

"Oh, bless you and your heart. Maybe she can be your new hobby to keep you out of trouble. She'll need to be walked and groomed and pampered and between that and your two jobs, you won't have time to get involved. Or at least that's what Burton told me when he suggested I ask you to keep her."

I would have laughed, but I was too tired to do more than smile. "She's in good hands. If you're in the area and want to visit her, give me a call. You have my number."

"Thank you, Tallie. I'll let you go. I see your man over there waving at you, and I don't want to keep you. A good life to you." She waved and I followed the line of her gaze.

"And a good new start to you, Marianne."

She hugged me and kept walking, eyeing the cake in the front window of the Bean before turning down a side street and getting into her maroon car.

I stepped into the café and was immediately caught in a huge hug. One that I wasn't sure who was giving it.

"Thank you," the man said and I recognized the voice from the recording on Eli's voicemail. The guy who was dying. "Thank you so much for finding out who my birth mother was."

"Okay." What else was I supposed to say?

Mama Shirley came around the corner and hugged me, too. I looked over her shoulder at Max, who just smiled at me.

"You brought a sheep into the fold, Tallie. I promise not to mention any old snafus anymore. We have one of our own back and now we can help him. Robbie is going to make it through this with the help of his family, aren't you, my love?"

Robbie smiled, and it clicked. If Burton's brother had fathered him, and Burton was Shirley's cousin, then Robbie had just stepped into a huge mess of family. He might survive the disease, but maybe not the overwhelming number of relatives who were going to come crashing down on his head. But he looked happy enough to deal with it, and Mama Shirley was beaming.

Okay then.

I finally got to Max. He hugged me hard. "I thought I asked you to wait for me."

"And I thought I had it all figured out." I snuggled in then looked up at him. "How'd you find me anyway?"

"When Annie carried you down to the creek your phone dropped in the grass. I used that GPS thing you find so amusing when Burton called to tell me he couldn't get ahold of you and your phone had cut out."

"The People Finder." I laughed and it was good. Maybe I'd have to write a glowing review for the thing.

"That's the one. Want to tell me about that talk across the street?" he raised an eyebrow and I figured Mama Shirley had been filling him in and so had Gina.

"I have a new dog."

Shirley snickered and so did Gina.

I was surprised to see her since my brother had become super-overprotective guy again. We won't go into how he'd reacted to her being knocked out. Let's just say that Jeremy was taking coddling to a whole new level.

Whatever they did was fine with me, though. They could dog sit when I went down to visit Max unless I could finally get him to consider moving up here. Maybe this would be my ace in the hole. I'd find out later after I enjoyed getting to know Robbie and finishing my coffee and my sticky bun.

Another case closed and this one had hit close to home, but it was all good. Maybe I *would* get a hobby. Convincing Max to move up here might be a good one.

Rhoda came running into the Bean. "Oh, Tallie, I was hoping I'd find you! I need your help! Can you and your young man fill in for the tour this afternoon? I'm sure I have a period costume that fits you. Paul is about Max's size. The couples don't want to cancel and take their money back. They want someone to lead them around town and show them all the wonders of our small community. I immediately thought of you."

Then again, I might want to move down to DC to escape all the people who thought of me first when it came time to solve problems that cropped up.

I agreed, of course I did, and only had to cajole Max a little bit to get him to put on the hose and buckle shoes that afternoon. He made a mighty fine colonist, if I did say so myself.

So, we'd stay. And I'd convince him to move up here with me and my cat and now my dog. And it would be good. I would avoid my dad's offer, move out of the apartment above the dead, and start working on my dreams. Whatever those were. At the moment, though, my one dream I was sure of stood in a brown wig with a ponytail, looking absolutely wonderful.

Time to get this show on the road. And I was all too happy that Max was on the road with me.

ACKNOWLEDGMENTS

Many, many, many thanks to all the fabulous people at Kensington for taking a chance on me. Esi, I had no idea what this journey would be like when you asked me to send you a hundred pages, but even with my imagination I would never have thought it would be this fantastic! Thank you.

And I have to give a shout-out to Funeral Bob at Myers-Buhrig Funeral Home—I would never have been able to do all this without you and your thoughtfulness, and your time. Thanks!

Don't miss the other books in
THE TALLIE GRAVER SERIES
by Misty Simon

Cremains of the Day

and

Grounds for Remorse

Available now from
Kensington Books,
wherever books are sold.

Connect with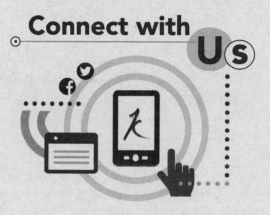

Visit us online at
KensingtonBooks.com
to read more from your favorite authors, see books
by series, view reading group guides, and more.

for sneak peeks, chances to win books and prize packs,
and to share your thoughts with other readers.

facebook.com/kensingtonpublishing
twitter.com/kensingtonbooks

Tell us what you think!

To share your thoughts, submit a review,
or sign up for our eNewsletters, please visit:
KensingtonBooks.com/TellUs.